Angel Fire

BY

GERRI HILL

Bella BOOKS

2014

Other Bella Books by Gerri Hill

Artist's Dream
At Seventeen
Behind the Pine Curtain
The Cottage
Coyote Sky
Dawn of Change
Devil's Rock
Gulf Breeze
Hell's Highway
Hunter's Way
In the Name of the Father
Keepers of the Cave
The Killing Room
Love Waits
The Midnight Moon
No Strings
One Summer Night
Partners
The Rainbow Cedar
The Scorpion
Sierra City
Snow Falls
Storms
The Target
Weeping Walls

About the Author

Gerri Hill has twenty-six published works, including the 2013 GCLS winner *Snow Falls*, 2011 and 2012 GCLS winners *Devil's Rock* and *Hell's Highway*, and the 2009 GCLS winner *Partners*, the last book in the popular Hunter Series, as well as the 2012 Lambda finalist *Storms*. Hill's love of nature and of being outdoors usually makes its way into her stories as her characters often find themselves in beautiful natural settings. When she isn't writing, Gerri and her longtime partner, Diane, keep busy at their log cabin in East Texas tending to their two vegetable gardens, orchard and five acres of piney woods. They share their lives with two Australian shepherds and an assortment of furry felines.

CHAPTER ONE

Tori Hunter leaned back in her camp chair and watched with amusement as her best friend attempted to get the fire going.

"O'Connor, what the hell are you doing?"

"Lighter fluid." Casey paused. "Unless you want to get your ass up and help."

"No, no. I'm fine. But after you blow that thing up, would you bring me a beer?"

Casey turned to her. "Are you going to get up and do *anything*?"

"I'm on vacation. I think that's what you promised me when I agreed to come out here, wasn't it? That you'd take care of everything and I could relax," Tori reminded her.

"Yeah, but as bossy as you are, I didn't think you could stand it."

"Bossy? *Me*?"

Casey gave her a crooked smile. "Oh, yeah, Hunter. You."

"Come on. I've mellowed in the last few years. That's what Sam says. Some people might even say I'm nice now."

Casey laughed. "Name me one of your colleagues who would use that word. And I mean current colleagues. You can't use John. You saved his life. He's got to say that."

Her current team flashed through her mind quickly and… okay. So maybe Casey had a point.

"Yeah. Thought so," Casey teased as she headed toward their rented RV, presumably to fetch the beer she'd requested.

Tori smiled at her, then took a deep breath of the fresh mountain air, so different from the city air she was used to. She had to admit, it was relaxing, this camping trip that Casey and Leslie had talked them into. She'd balked at first. A trip to New Mexico? In a rented motor home? For a whole damn week? No, not her thing. But Sam had thought it would be fun and Casey had badgered her enough that she finally agreed. Back in Dallas, the four of them hung out whenever their schedules allowed, which seemed to be less and less lately. Casey and Leslie still worked Homicide and Sam was still at CIU. Tori had moved on to the FBI a few years ago now. She would like to say she loved it, but the truth was, she missed Homicide and she missed working with Casey. But after what had happened to John Sikes, after the whole Patrick Doe thing, she needed a change. She hadn't even told Sam yet, but she was thinking about going back to the Dallas Police Department. That was one reason she'd agreed to this trip. She wanted time away to think things over and decide if she was ready to go back. She didn't want to get Sam's hopes up if she wasn't sure.

"Here you go, princess," Casey said as she handed Tori a bottle of beer.

"Thanks." Tori glanced toward the RV. "What are they doing in there?"

"Sam is making some sort of rice dish and Leslie is seasoning the chicken." Casey pulled her chair closer. "This is great, isn't it? We could be back home sweltering in the heat. September and it's still in the upper 90s there. That's crazy." She took a deep breath. "Instead, we're up here in the mountains. No humidity. It's nice and cool. And we're getting to see a little early fall color." She clanked her beer bottle against Tori's in a silent salute. "It's great up here, isn't it?"

"Yeah, it is." Tori took a swallow from her beer. "Thanks for making me do this."

"Yeah." Casey took a swallow of beer too. "You know, they want to go into Taos tomorrow. How about we let them go and you and I hike down to that trout stream the ranger was telling us about?"

Tori raised her eyebrows. "You think they'll go for it?"

Casey nodded and grinned. "Yeah. We'll just whine enough. They'll be glad to get rid of us."

"Well, it's been a while since we've been fishing."

"It's been a while since we've hung out," Casey reminded her. "That's why I thought this vacation would do us all good. You've been a little, well, cranky lately."

Tori laughed. "Cranky? *Me*?"

"You need to talk about something?" Casey offered.

Tori nodded. She'd met Casey by chance. Casey was still with Special Victims Unit back when they'd assigned her to Homicide to work a case. They'd hit it off immediately, something very rare for Tori. Back then, she didn't have any friends, only Sam. But she and Casey had clicked right away. She found it was as easy to talk to Casey as it was to Sam.

"I'm thinking of leaving the FBI," she said.

"Really? I thought you loved it."

Tori shrugged. "It was a nice change. I needed it."

"And now?"

"It's just goddamn politics all the time. I hate that part of it." She looked over at her. "Truth is, I miss Homicide. I miss the team."

"You want to come back?"

"Maybe. What do you think?"

"Oh, hell yeah, Hunter, that'd be great. You know Lieutenant Malone would find a spot for you, no problem. Maybe me and you, you know."

"You recently got a new partner though."

"Yeah, and I like him okay. I mean, he's not Leslie, don't get me wrong," she said with smile. "But I'm not really attached to him or anything. Besides, he thinks I talk too much."

Tori laughed. "Now that's a surprise."

"No. Seriously. You going to come back?"

"It's been on my mind a lot lately."

"What does Sam think?"

"I haven't told her. I wanted to be sure." She took another swallow of her beer. "Our schedules are so off, we don't have nearly as much time together anymore. I know she'd be thrilled if I went back."

"Yeah, we all would."

"We'll see. Career-wise, that'd be taking a step back, you know."

"Oh, please. You FBI types always think you're on the top of the world," Casey said with a laugh.

"That's because we are, O'Connor."

They looked up as a truck sped their way, then slammed to a stop. It was a dusty green Forest Service truck and a ranger got out, practically running toward them.

"You're law enforcement, right?" he asked quickly. "They told me you were. I got a situation."

"A situation?" Casey asked. "We're kinda out of our jurisdiction, you know. I'm Dallas PD." Casey pointed at Tori. "Hunter here is FBI. I guess maybe that would fly."

"What's going on?" Tori asked.

"I got a distress call from the wife of one of my rangers," he said as he twisted his hands together nervously. "This is his day off. She said someone was in their house, that he had a gun. I heard shots and the line went dead."

"Sheriff's department?"

"Yeah, I called them, but they got a huge mess down on Highway 64. They got five cars involved, but they got gunshot victims too," he explained. "They're sending someone up here as soon as they can, but I got a bad feeling. I mean, I heard shots on the phone. I need somebody right now."

Tori looked at Casey. "I guess we could go take a look."

"Yeah. Okay." Casey got up. "I'll get our weapons and tell Sam and Les."

But they had already come outside. Sam walked up to her, her eyes questioning. "Everything okay?"

"I think so. He wants us to check out something. Possible home invasion," she said. "It's going to be a little while before the sheriff's department gets here. Thought we'd go take a look."

"Okay. We'll hold off dinner then."

"We'll be right back." She hesitated a second as she looked at Sam, her gut telling her not to leave for some reason. She felt a bit embarrassed with the ranger watching, so she shook it off and pulled Sam into a quick hug. "Be right back," she whispered into her ear.

"Be careful."

"Always."

CHAPTER TWO

"He's got two daughters," he said as he turned onto a small dirt road that cut into the forest. "I don't know their ages. One is in high school. The other is, oh, I don't know, ten or eleven, I guess."

The road opened into a rocky clearing, and a small log cabin came into view. It blended well with the trees and rocks, and Tori had time to think how appealing it looked. But the ranger slammed on his brakes and her gaze was brought to the body lying on the road.

"Oh, shit," Casey murmured.

She and Casey got out. Tori pointed to the ranger. "You stay here."

He nodded, his eyes wide. "That…oh, God, that's the oldest daughter."

They walked forward. Casey squatted down, touching the girl's neck. She looked up at Tori and shook her head.

"Shot. Back of the head."

"Looks like she was running toward the road," Tori said quietly, her eyes on the house. She pulled out her weapon and Casey did the same. Tori motioned with her head to the left and Casey headed that way. Tori moved slowly to the right, listening. But it was quiet. Too quiet. There wasn't even a bird to be heard.

Casey pointed around the side, indicating she was going to the back of the house. Tori nodded, then walked up on the porch. The front door was ajar. A bloody hand print was smeared on the side. She pushed it open slowly, the hinges squeaking as the door swung inward. A man was on the floor, face down. Blood pooled around his head. She stepped over him, going into the living room.

She heard Casey enter from the back. The kitchen, she assumed. She took the hallway, opening the bedroom doors. All three were empty and looked undisturbed.

"Clear," she called.

"Clear," Casey called back.

Tori went back to the living room and into the kitchen. Casey met her at the door.

"Found the wife," she said. "Dead."

Tori nodded. "Yeah. Got a male by the front door. I assume the husband."

"The wife was shot in the face," Casey said. "Could have been while she was on the phone."

"Bedrooms looked undisturbed," she said. "Maybe the younger daughter wasn't home."

"Or maybe he took her." Casey shook her head. "What the fuck happened here, Hunter?"

"I don't know. It's like they were executed. All shot in the head." She headed back to the door. "Let me get the ranger in here to make a positive ID."

* * *

With a little coaxing, Sam got the campfire going again. She would make a point to let Casey know she'd done it without lighter fluid too.

"Only three days and police work comes into play," Leslie said as she sat down beside her.

"I know. We all needed a break. I hope it's nothing serious." Sam leaned closer. "And now that we're alone, tell me about this house you're looking at."

Leslie's eye lit up as she smiled. "We've been talking about buying for a few months now. And of course, the first thing Casey did was look in your area."

"That would be great, you know. It seems like it's so hard for all of us to get together lately. I know Tori misses spending time with Casey."

"Casey too," Leslie said. "I don't want to crowd you, though. If Casey had her way, we'd move next door."

Sam laughed. "And I think that would be fine with Tori too."

"What do you think about—"

"Help! Help us!"

They turned, seeing a man dragging a young girl. She was covered in blood. They jumped up, hurrying toward him.

"What happened?" Leslie asked as she took hold of the girl.

Sam was about to do the same when the man pulled out a gun, using it to smash against Leslie's head. Leslie fell limply to the ground, taking the girl with her.

"No!" Sam yelled, turning, grabbing the man's hand, but he twisted away, wrapping an arm tight around her neck and pressing the barrel of his gun against her temple.

"Don't think I won't shoot you."

Sam drew in quick, short breaths of air, but she stopped struggling against his hold. She turned her head, glancing to the ground where Leslie lay. She was bleeding from a wound to her head, unconscious. The girl who lay beside her appeared to be dead.

"Who...who are you?"

"Not your concern." He pulled her roughly after him, his arm still holding her tightly around her neck. Up the steps of the RV they went, and Sam's eyes darted to a drawer beside the television. Her weapon was there, but if she disabled him, she wasn't sure she could get to it in time.

He flung her down on the small sofa, the gun aimed at her head. "Put some jeans on. Hiking boots too."

She frowned. "What? Why?"

"I am not in the mood for stupid questions. Do it," he yelled.

They had flipped a coin for sleeping arrangements, and she and Tori had won the bedroom as opposed to the fold-out sofa. She got up slowly, holding her hands up. She pointed into the bedroom. "My…my clothes are in there."

"You have fifteen seconds."

She had her back to him as she took her shorts off and slipped on jeans. Her hands were trembling slightly as she found her hiking socks and put them on, her mind whirling as she tried to figure out what to do.

"Hurry."

She barely had time to put her boots on before he grabbed her arm and pulled her up. "Sweatshirt and a jacket."

"Where…where are you taking me?"

"You don't get to ask questions."

She was a cop, yet she felt so helpless. If this was Tori, the man would already be dead. But she wasn't Tori and she wasn't about to try to disarm him. If she failed, she had no doubt he would kill her. So she did as he said, only it was Tori's sweatshirt she grabbed instead of her own. That brought some comfort to her as she slipped it over her head.

He pulled her back outside and pushed her down to the ground. She looked over at Leslie, who still hadn't moved.

"On your knees," he said. "Cross your ankles. Hands behind your head."

She did as she was told, her body trembling from fear as she raised her hands over her head and locked her fingers together. Was he going to execute her? No. He'd had her change clothes for a reason. He ripped down the rope they'd strung up to hang their towels on to dry. A sheath on his leg produced a large knife, and he cut the rope in half. He walked over to her, then jerked her up.

"Hold your hands out."

Her eyes were locked on the knife, and she did as she was told, knowing once she was tied up any thought of escape would be gone. Her bound hands were tied to a nearby tree.

He took the remaining rope and tied Leslie's hands to those of the girl's. Sam stared helplessly as Leslie was tied up.

"Is she…is she dead?"

"The girl? Yeah. Your friend here, no." He held his knife up. "Should I finish her off?"

"Please…don't," Sam whispered.

"And if I spare her, what do I get in return?"

"What…what do you want?"

He said nothing. He walked back toward the road from where he'd come. For a moment, Sam thought he was leaving. But he bent down, pulling out a large backpack from behind a tree. He slipped it over his shoulders and headed back toward her. He paused at the water spigot, moving his hands under the stream of water. Washing off blood. When he looked at her, Sam averted her eyes. She heard him walk near and he untied the rope from the tree.

"Lift your arms."

She did, trying to decide if she was strong enough to fight him. He took the excess rope that dangled from her wrists and pulled it up roughly, halting her thoughts. He wrapped it around her waist, then tied to around his own.

"There. Now we're attached. No escape." He tightened the rope a little more. "And in case you're wondering, I can kill as quickly with my bare hands as I can with my gun or knife."

Sam met his eyes fully for the first time. She expected evil. She expected insanity. Instead, she found neither. Intelligent brown eyes looked back at her.

"What…what is it that you want?"

"A hostage." He held up his knife again. "In exchange, I won't cut your friend's throat."

CHAPTER THREE

Tori ran her hands through her hair, noting that they were trembling. Her stomach was in knots and her chest hurt. *Sam… please.*

"Tori?"

She turned, meeting Casey's concerned eyes. She nodded. "How's Les?"

"They're going to take her to the hospital," Casey said. "She said a man came out of the woods dragging the girl. They didn't know she was dead. When they went to help, he hit her with something. When she came to, she was tied to the girl." She paused. "Sam was gone."

"Yeah. Okay."

"You called your people, right?"

"Yeah. I'm supposed to wait for a call from some guy named Murdock." She let her frustration show. "Goddamn, O'Connor. The bastard took Sam and I'm supposed to *wait*? What the hell?"

"What else can you do?"

"What can I do?" she asked loudly. "I can fucking go after her, that's what." She headed to the motorhome as if to do just that, but Casey grabbed her arm.

"It's dark, Tori. Come on. Where you gonna go, huh? Head north?" Then she pointed into the woods. "Or maybe head out there into the woods somewhere? I think that's west. Hell, Hunter, or go south. Maybe he went that way. Or maybe he had a car and took the highway. Nobody knows where he went. The sheriff's department is up to their eyeballs in crime scenes. They've got the house here. They've got the accident on the highway where four people were shot. I heard one of them say they found a car south of Taos with two bodies, both shot at close range. They're thinking that may be linked to the accident. So you've got to wait, Hunter."

"Goddamn, O'Connor," she muttered, knowing Casey was right.

"You can't just head out into the woods like a crazy woman, Tori," Casey said. "We wait for a team to get here."

"He killed that family like it was nothing," she said, snapping her fingers. "What the hell do you think he'll do to Sam?"

"He took her because he needs her. If he wanted her dead, she would be. So would Leslie." Casey released her arm. "Now, anything disturbed inside?" she asked, motioning to the motorhome.

Tori swallowed down the lump in her throat. "She changed into jeans. Her shorts were on the floor. Hiking boots missing." She closed her eyes. "And my sweatshirt."

"Her weapon?"

Tori shook her head. "It's still in the drawer. So is her cell." She flicked her gaze to the approaching paramedic.

"Excuse me, but we're heading out," he said to Casey. "Did you want to go?"

Casey looked at her and Tori nodded. "Go on, O'Connor. Be with Leslie."

Casey walked over to her and hugged her quickly. "Don't do anything stupid, Hunter. Wait for the team."

Tori managed a small smile. "I'll keep that in mind."

Casey left and Tori turned her gaze back to the ever-darkening forest. She closed her eyes. *Sam…please be okay.* She had never felt so helpless as she did in that moment. She wasn't used to feeling helpless and she wasn't used to waiting. She was used to doing.

She returned her gaze to the trees beyond the motorhome. That was where he took her. She didn't know how she knew, but she felt it in her gut, in her heart. That was where he took Sam. She took a few steps in that direction, then stopped. She knew it would be futile to set out alone.

And alone was what she was. She stared up into the night sky, feeling as lonely at that moment as she had when her family was killed when she was a child. Maybe more so. She knew Sam meant everything to her, knew Sam was the most important thing in her life. She knew that. But she didn't count on the complete emptiness she felt at her absence.

She heard a twig snap, and she turned, surprised to see Casey heading toward her.

"What the hell, O'Connor?"

Casey shrugged and stepped close to her, their shoulders touching.

"You're supposed to be with Les."

Casey shook her head. "Right now, I think you need me more than she does."

"Oh, hell, Casey. You need to be with her."

"I need to be with you." Casey bumped her shoulder. "Besides, she made me stay."

Tori nodded. Yeah, Leslie would do that. "Okay."

"Come on," Casey said. "We got that bottle of scotch. I think we need a drink."

Tori's gaze drifted back toward the forest. "Yeah. Okay." She looked at Casey. "But I don't want to talk, O'Connor."

"Hell, we're not going to talk. We're going to drink and wait for your people to call you."

CHAPTER FOUR

Andrea held her tight as Cameron collapsed on top of her. Their skin was damp and they both struggled to catch their breath.

"Making love in the afternoon...it's the best thing ever," Cameron murmured against her neck.

Andrea laughed quietly. "I thought pizza was," she teased, referring to the frozen treat she'd fixed for a late lunch. They hadn't been anywhere near a pizza place for eight days. Cameron's love of the pie brought out the only frozen one they had left.

"It was pretty good for frozen." Cameron rolled off her and took a deep breath. "I love you, Andi."

Andrea smiled as she leaned up on an elbow. Those words came easily to Cameron now. "I love you too." She reached out and lightly traced the scar that slashed across Cameron's breast. She watched as Cameron's nipple turned rigid. "And you're right. Making love in the afternoon is kinda nice. Although I think the afternoon is well behind us," she said as she glanced out the window, seeing nothing but darkness.

Cameron rolled her head toward her. "Are you tired of this life yet?"

Andrea shook her head. "No. I love all the traveling that we do."

"And being cramped in this motorhome?"

"I don't feel cramped." Andrea studied her. Yes, they'd done a lot of traveling in the last year. Murdock had kept them plenty busy, and they'd hit nearly every western state except New Mexico. She didn't mind the constant movement. And she knew Cameron was used to it, not only from growing up in a military family but being in the military herself. But there was a look on Cameron's face that Andrea had not seen before. "Are you tired of it?"

Cameron took her hand and brought it to her lips, kissing it softly. "I sometimes think it would be nice to settle somewhere. Maybe do something normal."

"Tired of the FBI?"

Cameron met her eyes. "We see so much…so much crap, Andi. Death. Heartache. Tears." She looked away. "We don't see laughter very often."

"No, we don't." Andrea squeezed her hand. "But if you're ready to settle down somewhere, we should start thinking about it. Although I wouldn't even know where to land. I loved Sedona and the sheriff's department," she said. "I don't think I'd ever want to go back to a large city and a large police force. Talk about no laughter."

"So maybe we'll settle in a little mountain town where they need a couple of very experienced and highly trained ex-FBI agents," Cameron said with a grin.

Andrea matched her smile. "We seem to land in Colorado a lot, don't we?"

"Yeah, we tend to come back here between cases. Maybe—"

But Cameron's phone interrupted her and they recognized Murdock's ringtone.

"Haven't heard from him in a week," Andrea said.

Cameron nodded as she fumbled for the phone. "Ross," she said in her most professional tone, causing Andrea to smile. If he'd called five minutes earlier, she'd have been breathless as she answered.

Andrea's smile faded as Cameron looked at her.

"I'll log on right now. Give me a second," Cameron said. "We're...outside."

Andrea got out of bed, trying to find her jeans. Cameron had pulled on her T-shirt, not bothering with her bra.

"What's up?" Andrea asked as she found her shirt.

"He wants us on video. All he said was 'a hell of a situation,'" Cameron said as she pulled her jeans on. "I'm going to log in." She paused. "How do I look?"

Andrea walked closer, running her fingers through Cameron's hair to tame it. "You need a cut."

Cameron leaned closer and kissed her. "You should probably check the mirror before you come out."

Andrea hurried into the small bathroom, smiling. Her hair was a tangled mess. She splashed water on her face, then took a brush and brought some semblance of order to it. She took a moment to finger it, wondering what Cameron would say if she got it cut shorter. Well, now wasn't the time to think about it. She scooped Lola up as she walked into the living area of the motorhome. Lola purred loudly as Andrea nuzzled her black fur.

She sat the cat down when Murdock's face came up on Cameron's laptop. He didn't bother with pleasantries.

"Have you had a chance to catch the news today?"

Cameron looked at Andrea and they shook their heads. "I try to avoid it as much as possible," Cameron said.

"Well, it's been a whirlwind of a day. We're just now piecing everything together," he said. He looked at a sheet of paper he held in his hand. "We had an armored-car heist in Santa Fe, New Mexico, late morning. Four men, armed with assault rifles. This company stocked ATMs. Estimated net haul is three million," he said. "Two guards killed. The armored car was abandoned about a mile away. Money gone. Three hours later, two of the men were found shot dead. Their bodies were found in what we assume was the getaway car, south of Taos, New Mexico. Midafternoon, there was a traffic accident east of Taos on Highway 64. Five vehicles involved. Drivers in two of the vehicles had been shot. Four shooting victims total at that scene."

He put the paper down. "And that's only the beginning. A family of four was murdered in their home, off Highway 64, going toward Eagle Nest. That's about thirty miles or so from Taos. The family was that of a Forest Service personnel. With the sheriff's department tied up with the accident, the ranger who took the initial call from the wife commandeered the service of an FBI agent who happened to be camping near there. They found the husband, wife and one daughter dead at the scene. The other daughter was taken, presumably already dead, as a decoy. She was used to summon help from nearby campers." He paused. "And now we have a hostage situation. Or at least we think we do."

"That's a lot going on, Murdock. I'm assuming everything is related. Got IDs yet?" Cameron asked.

He nodded. "Video surveillance at the armored car company caught all four men. That's how we identified the two dead outside of Taos. Another man is believed to be one of the victims in the accident on 64. That leaves one of the four remaining. Identified as Angel Figueroa. Ring a bell?"

Cameron's eyes widened. "Angel?" She slowly shook her head. "He's not a bank robber, Murdock. He's a goddamn sniper."

"I know who he is, but I'm telling you what we know so far. Ballistics isn't back yet, but we're pretty certain everything is linked."

Cameron turned quickly to Andrea. "Angel and I, we were in the military together. He was on my team for a while. He was the second best sniper in the group," she explained.

Andrea didn't need to ask who the best was.

"The last I heard of Angel, he was a mercenary of sorts, still in the Middle East," Cameron said to Murdock. "He was paid well, I assume. Why come back here, to a small city in New Mexico and pull a heist?"

"Maybe he was low on cash. We're putting together a profile on him now, tracking his whereabouts since he got out of the military."

Cameron shook her head. "He's a hired killer, nothing more. There's got to be something to it other than just a robbery."

"Well, I do have more, actually," he said. "The FBI agent who was at the scene, she's from Dallas. She was camping with three others, all three are with Dallas PD. They were camping in the Santa Fe National Forest at one of the campgrounds there. The woman missing is Samantha Kennedy, one of the three cops."

"Why do you think it's a hostage situation? That's not Angel's style."

"He brought a dead girl with him as a decoy, got the women to help him. He coldcocked one of them. When she came to, she was bound at the wrists, tied to the dead girl. The other woman, Kennedy, was missing."

"What about the fourth one?" Andrea asked.

"She was with the FBI agent." Murdock looking slightly uncomfortable. "I believe the four of them were…well, I assume they are two…couples. Well, I know they are. Agent Tori Hunter—Kennedy is her partner, as I hear it."

"Manhunt underway?"

"No. The local authorities had their hands full trying to process everything. They've kept the area secure from where we assume Kennedy was taken. He'd taken the family's car there and stashed it in the woods. Knowing what we know about Angel, my gut tells me he's on foot. The deputies there don't seem to be in agreement. They think he may be on the highway."

"No. Angel would have headed into the woods," she said. "That was his training."

"Yeah, I know. But because he's pretty much shot up their county down there, the locals want him bad. I don't even have the final death count. Ten or eleven," he said. "They've got roadblocks setup on the highway in both directions. They're planning on bringing in dogs in the morning to the campsite there. Unless I can convince them you'd do a better job of it."

"You want me to track Angel Figueroa?" Cameron asked. "He's good. He's very good."

"Yes. He's a survivalist. Who better to go after him than you?"

"I've been out of the military a few years now, Murdock."

"I'm well aware, Agent Ross. But you're it. Pack your bags."

"I've got backcountry gear for me, but not Andrea," she said. "And we'll need rations."

"I'll have gear there for you when you land."

"Land? What about the rig? What about our truck? What about Lola?"

"Lola? Your cat is not my concern. The rig and your fancy truck are my concern. Someone is on the way right now to your location. He'll drive the rig and pull your truck to New Mexico. Get to Durango. There'll be a plane waiting. There won't be much time to rest, I'm afraid. I want you on-site at daybreak. As you said, Angel is nothing more than a killer. When he no longer needs his hostage, he'll eliminate her."

"So where's the money? Three million is a lot of cash," Andrea said.

"We're going over surveillance cameras in Santa Fe and Taos. Since he's on foot and the vehicles are clean, we assume he stashed the money somewhere in the area."

"Have you ID'd the accomplices?"

"We've ID'd the two bodies found in Taos. Both ex-military, although there's no obvious link to Angel. Their paths didn't cross while deployed. Both were honorably discharged last year." He paused. "Find him, Cameron. Dead or alive, I don't care. What I do care about is that you bring Samantha Kennedy back safely. This is a rescue mission, first and foremost."

"Okay, Murdock. We're on it," Cameron said.

"I'll be in touch."

When the screen went blank, Cameron closed up the laptop. "Not much warning." She shook her head. "And a hell of a lot happening."

"Tori Hunter? That name is familiar. Wasn't she on the Patrick Doe case back in Dallas?"

"Yeah. We spoke with her, didn't we?"

"I think so." Andrea sat down beside her and pulled Lola into her lap. "Well, this assignment will be different."

"Yeah. It's been a while since I've done any tracking like this." Cameron sighed. "I'm going to miss the rig though."

Andrea laughed. "You mean you're going to miss your toys."

"Yeah. Remind me to lock the computer room up tight." She leaned forward and kissed Andrea lightly on the lips. "I had a very nice afternoon."

Andrea smiled against her lips. "Good. So did I." She brushed the sandy-blond hair away from Cameron's eyes. "And you *really* need a trim."

"I know. Looks like it will have to wait though."

CHAPTER FIVE

Sam sat on the ground where he'd shoved her, contemplating making a run for it. It was the first time she'd been untied from him since they'd left the campground. Her hands, however, remained bound. She watched intently as he got a small fire going. If she did try to run, where would she go? Her hands were bound. He would catch her in an instant. He wasn't a big man. Not much taller than herself. But he appeared muscular. Fit. His hair was dark and cut very short, military style. His clothes—black—and accessories—gun holster and knife sheath strapped to his thigh—also suggested military.

"Come closer if you're cold," he said brusquely. "That's what it's for. I won't let it burn for long."

She had no idea what time it was, but they had walked for a while after darkness fell, presumably to put as much distance between them and the campground. And Tori. But she was cold so she scooted closer to the fire, holding her hands out to the warmth.

"My…my name is Samantha," she finally said.

He glanced over at her but made no comment.

"Can I at least know your name?"

"Why?"

"So that when we talk, I can address you," she said.

He gave a quick smile. "What makes you think we're going to talk?" His smile faded. "I'm a killer, remember? When I don't need you anymore…well, you won't need to know my name."

She watched him as he opened up an MRE, another indication that he had ties to the military—meals ready to eat. Her stomach rumbled, but when he tried to hand her the meal she shook her head. "I'm not hungry."

"We're not eating for pleasure, we're eating for fuel. We'll have a long hike tomorrow. Now eat."

She took the package from him, staring at the brown mess that was supposed to be a beef stew. She grimaced at the taste and quickly chased it down with the water he'd given her.

"Easy on the water," he warned. "It's limited."

She took another bite of the stew. "Why…why did you kill that young girl?"

"We'll get along much better if you just keep quiet and stop asking questions."

"I'm sorry." She met his eyes in the firelight. "It's…well… I'm…I'm a cop," she said. "I ask questions."

"A cop?" He looked at her skeptically. "You think pretending to be a cop is going to change the outcome? I hate cops."

She swallowed nervously. "Dallas Police Department."

He stared at her for a long moment. "My hostage is a cop? And I suppose you're going to say your friend is too?"

"Her name is Leslie. Yes. She's a cop too."

"Great. And you two…are you like a couple or something?"

Sam shook her head. "Leslie is one of my best friends." She took another bite of the stew, forcing herself to eat it. "We were there—vacation—with our partners though. Tori. Tori Hunter." Just saying the name out loud brought her some comfort. "She's my…my partner. She's with the FBI," she added.

His laugh surprised her. "My hostage is a cop and her lesbian lover is with the FBI. Wow," he said dryly. He leaned closer. "And just where was this FBI agent when I showed up?"

"She and Casey went with one of the rangers. There was a...a shooting." She paused. "I suppose that was you."

"Yeah, I suppose it was." He shook his head again. "A cop. Jesus," he said almost to himself. He got up then, startling her. "Do I need to tie you up?"

She held her hands up, which were still bound. "What do you mean?"

"Do I need to worry about you running off into the woods? I'm not in the mood to chase you."

She looked past their little campfire, seeing nothing but blackness. Where would she go? She turned back to him and shook her head.

"No, I don't suppose you would run," he said. "A mountain lion would get you and have you for dinner before I could find you."

Sam stared at him blankly. *Mountain lion?* "I won't run."

He went to his backpack and untied what she assumed was a tent. He shook it out away from the fire, then quickly assembled it. She closed her eyes, silently begging for Tori to find her. She had no doubt that Tori was out right now, searching for her. Although she was a little discouraged that she'd heard no helicopters in the air earlier. Surely someone was searching for her. Of course, it was nearly dark when he'd taken her. Maybe they weren't searching for her yet. Maybe they would wait until morning. What appetite she had vanished and she put the so-called stew down. She couldn't swallow another bite.

"Finish it," he said.

"It's...it's atrocious," she said, causing him to laugh.

"Yeah, I know. But you get used to it."

Sam looked up at him. "Ex-military?"

His smile vanished. "Eat it. Like I said, it's not for pleasure, it's for fuel."

She picked up the stew again, wondering if she could force down any more of it. One more bite and she felt her stomach revolt. She put it down again. "I can't."

"Suit yourself," he said.

He picked it up and, using her spoon, finished it off. He folded the empty container and put it into a small trash bag where he'd put his earlier. This he tied to a rope and swung it over a tree limb a short distance from their fire. She knew it was to prevent wild animals from finding it, which made her wonder what else was around besides mountain lions. Bears?

He came back over to the fire and kicked dirt on it, putting it out. Her world plunged into darkness then, and she squinted into the shadows. She looked overhead, but there was no moon.

"Come on."

He grabbed her roughly and jerked her to her feet. She had a moment of panic as he was about to shove her inside the small tent.

"Wait," she said. "I...I need to pee."

He sighed. "Yes, I suppose you do." He pointed at her. "Stay here."

She did as she was told, waiting as he ducked into the tent. He came out with a roll of toilet paper. He wordlessly handed it to her, then pulled on the rope, leading her behind a tree.

"You're going to...*watch*?"

"You're testing my patience," he said.

It was dark. He wouldn't be able to see anything, she reasoned. She let out a heavy breath. "Can you at least turn around?"

He was silent and didn't move for the longest time. Then, finally, the rope loosened and he let go of the slack and moved around the tree.

"Thank you."

"Hurry up."

She didn't know if she was more embarrassed or humiliated at that moment. She squatted down beside the tree, hoping he wasn't listening. At that thought, she rolled her eyes. Him listening to her pee was the least of her worries.

"Bring the toilet paper with you."

"What? Gross."

"Pick it up."

The tone of his voice told her not to argue. She waited while he lowered the trash bag and she put the toilet paper in after he'd opened it. He then repeated the process of hanging it back in the tree.

Without another word, he jerked her hands and pulled her toward the tent. Panic set in again as he shoved her inside. She was his hostage. He could do what he pleased. But she closed her eyes, vowing to fight him. She would not go through that again. She opened her eyes when she heard a quiet click and saw that he'd turned on a small flashlight. Their eyes met and he frowned slightly. She wondered what look she had on her face to cause that.

"I only have the one sleeping bag," he said. "Use your coat for cover. It gets cold at night."

He took the rope that was tied around her wrists and tied it to his arm. "I'm a light sleeper. Don't do anything stupid. Having a hostage helps my cause, but only a little. I'll kill you in a second if you try anything."

"Why do you need a hostage?"

"Because they're less likely to come after me with guns blazing, that's why."

"Wouldn't it be easier for you to disappear if you were by yourself?"

He sighed. "Goodnight."

She lay on her back, eyes wide open. How could she possibly sleep? She let out a quiet sigh of her own. How could this be happening to her? One minute, she and Leslie were discussing houses and the next, she was tied to a madman with a gun. And a knife, she reminded herself. She thought back over it all. Could she have done something? Should she have tried to get her weapon from the drawer? Should she have fought him? And on the heels of that, was Leslie okay? Was Tori okay? She could imagine how Tori was feeling. She pitied poor Casey, who had to put up with her. This brought a quick smile to her face. But it faded just as quickly.

She was in a tent in the middle of nowhere, tied to a man with a gun.

CHAPTER SIX

Cameron stepped out of the truck, her gaze going first to the small motorhome, then to her right where crime scene tape was wrapped around a group of trees. The yellow tape nearly glowed from the truck's headlights. She slid her heavy backpack to the ground.

"How did he get here?" she asked the sheriff's deputy who had escorted them here. Murdock had said something about a car.

"The family's car. We found it ditched down the road there, about two hundred yards."

"Give me some kind of timeline, if you can," she said.

"Sure." He pulled out a small notepad from his shirt pocket, then walked into the light from his truck. "Call came in about the shooting at six twenty. The ranger came over here, took Agent Hunter and O'Connor—she's with Dallas PD—with him to the scene. They got back here at seven ten."

"That's when they found the girl tied to the other police officer?" Andrea asked.

"Yes, ma'am. They called it in. Nothing was disturbed. There was evidence that Kennedy changed clothes and took a jacket." He looked at his notes. "Hunter said she was wearing shorts when they left them. The shorts were in the bedroom and jeans and hiking boots were missing."

"Nice of him to let her change," Andrea said.

"It would just slow him down if she wasn't equipped for hiking." Her gaze slid to the still-dark forest. "How far he'll go is anybody's guess."

"Where is Agent Hunter?" Andrea asked.

"Yeah, she's in there," he said, pointing to the motorhome. "She's not real friendly. The other one, O'Connor, she's nice."

"You got our gear?" Cameron asked.

"Yes, it's in the back of my truck."

"I'm going to go check it out," Cameron said to Andrea. She motioned with her head to the motorhome. "I'll let you talk to Hunter."

Andrea nodded and Cameron went around to the back of the truck. She let the tailgate down, then frowned. There were two packs, not just one. She pulled one closer to her and unzipped it, finding rations, two containers of water, some toiletries and little else. There was a sleeping bag and a tent strapped to the outside. She pulled over the other one, and it was equipped the same.

"Bare bones, Murdock," she murmured. And as if saying his name was a signal, her phone rang. "Why two packs?" she asked immediately when she answered. "I told you I had my own."

"And good morning to you too, Agent Ross. I trust you made it safely."

"Just got here," she said. "It's not daylight yet." She paused. "Two packs?"

"Yes. Well, Agent Hunter will accompany you."

"The hell she will," Cameron said loudly. "I won't have time to babysit."

"She's a trained agent, Cameron."

"Andrea and I work alone. I don't need her."

"I don't suppose you do. But you know who the hostage is."

"All the more reason for her not to go. This can't be personal."

He sighed. "Yeah. Well, I tried that approach with her too. And short of locking her up, there's no way to keep her from joining you."

Cameron glanced at the motorhome where she heard Andrea talking. "Come on, Murdock. You issue her an order. If she doesn't follow it, file insubordination and haul her off."

"Of course, Agent Ross, you know all about insubordination, don't you?"

"Come on, Murdock."

"Look, I already tried that. She threatened to quit the FBI and follow you anyway. Now if you can talk her into staying behind, fine. Use your charm on her," he said with a laugh. "But there's gear there for her to join you. She's a trained agent," he said again.

"Jesus, Murdock, this is not a great way to start a mission."

"And we don't have time to argue about it. The best we can do is hope Kennedy slows Angel down enough for you to catch up. Now, do you want air support? The locals are chomping at the bit to go after him. They've got a helicopter ready to go."

"No. Not yet. Let me get a feel for where he's going. Besides, we both know he can hide from a damn helicopter. Angel Figueroa is no amateur."

"If he was alone, sure. Maybe not with a hostage. But you make the call. You check in with me and let me know your progress."

"That's assuming I can find his trail," she said.

"I have no doubt that you will."

The call ended and she pocketed her phone. She looked to the sky and saw the first signs of dawn. She headed toward the motorhome. Now the fun part. No way in hell was she letting Agent Hunter go with them.

* * *

Tori looked up as the other woman approached. She could tell by the look on her face that she was not happy.

"I'm Special Agent Ross. Who is Hunter?"

"I'm Hunter," Tori said. She motioned to Casey. "This is O'Connor. Dallas PD."

Agent Sullivan stepped forward with a slightly amused expression. "Cameron...this is Tori and Casey," she said, pointing to each of them.

Agent Ross nodded. "I understand your...your colleague was injured."

Casey's eyebrows shot up. "Colleague? Is that what we're calling it now?" She gave Agent Ross the sarcastic smile Tori knew well. "My *partner*, Leslie, is doing fine. In fact, I'm heading to the hospital as soon as you guys take off."

"Good." Ross turned to Tori. "And I imagine you're going with her then?"

Tori shook her head. "As I told your man Murdock, I'm going with you."

Ross narrowed her eyes. "The hell you are."

Tori glared right back. "Yeah, the hell I am."

Ross sighed. "Look, Hunter, you don't have experience in this. We do. Let us do our job."

"I'm going with you."

"Goddamn it, Hunter, I don't have time to argue with you. They've got at least a two-hour head start on us, provided he stopped at full dark. It may be three hours. Do you know how long it's going to take to make up that time?" Ross shook her head. "You're not going."

"I'm not going to slow you down."

"You're not going," Ross said again.

"The hell I'm not," Tori said loudly. She pointed out to the woods. "That's my goddamn life out there."

"Then trust us to bring her back."

"I don't trust anyone but me," Tori said emphatically as she pointed at her chest.

Cameron stepped closer. "I said no."

Tori walked closer too. They were nearly nose to nose. "I don't care what you say. I'm fucking going with you."

Agent Sullivan put an arm between them. "Cameron."

"What?" she asked sharply.

Sullivan gave Tori a quick, somewhat apologetic smile, before glancing at Ross. "Can I speak with you for a minute?"

Tori was shocked at the change in Ross's demeanor as she nodded. When they walked away, Tori turned to Casey.

"I don't like her. At all."

Casey grinned. "I'm going to guess that the feeling is mutual." She motioned to Ross and Sullivan who were speaking in quiet voices. "Looks like we're not the only ones with *colleagues*."

Tori nodded. "Les is getting discharged, right?"

"Yeah."

"What are you going to do?"

"I guess we're going to come back here and wait," Casey said.

But Tori shook her head. "No. You guys take this thing and head back to Dallas. You don't need to wait here. I don't know how long it'll be."

"I don't want to leave you here, Tori. You might need me."

"If I need you, I'll call you. And you'll come, I know you will."

"I can't just leave, Tori. Sam is out there."

"And we're going to find her. I know that." She touched her heart. "I feel that."

Casey's expression softened and Tori found herself in a tight hug. "I love you."

Tori closed her eyes as she hugged Casey back. "I love you too."

They stepped apart quickly and Tori met her eyes. "God, I'm glad no one was here to witness that," she murmured.

They turned when Agent Sullivan approached. Tori raised her eyebrows questioningly.

"Grab your gear. There's a backpack you can use."

Tori let out a relieved breath. "Thank you." Her gaze followed Ross as she walked the perimeter of their site. "I won't slow you down."

CHAPTER SEVEN

The sun was barely up, yet Sam trudged behind him, her hands still bound. The rope, like yesterday, was tied around his waist. They were climbing higher and the junipers and scrub brush were being replaced with pine trees and other large conifers. The morning was cool and crisp, and she wished she had better company to enjoy it with. Her stomach rumbled just then, and she longed for a cup of coffee and breakfast. A big breakfast. Scrambled eggs, bacon, toast…the works. Maybe pancakes too. Oh, like those fluffy ones they got at Mike's Diner. That would be good right about now.

"Hungry?"

God, could he read her mind?

"I heard your stomach," he explained. "I told you to eat the stew."

"Yes," she said. "But I couldn't eat it. I was close to throwing up what I'd already eaten."

He slowed his pace. "We'll stop in a bit. Down the next ridge, we'll dip into the canyon. There's a stream there. We'll fill up our water bottles and get something to eat."

"A stream? You've been out this way before?"

He didn't answer.

"You know, you never did tell me your name."

"I thought I explained that."

"What's it going to hurt to tell me your name?"

Again, silence. She sighed, letting it go. She looked behind her, wondering if someone—Tori—was already on their trail. Surely. Yes, surely they were. But how much time did she have? How long before he felt safe without her? She tried not to think about that. Instead, she looked around her, not really seeing the beauty of the tall pine trees that they were hiking among. Because she wasn't really hiking. Not really, she thought, as her gaze went to the rope linking her with her captive. Well, if someone was following, she wanted to make sure they could find their trail. She kicked over an occasional rock, hoping he wouldn't get suspicious.

When he stopped suddenly, she bumped into him from the back. She took a step away from him and cocked her head, listening like he was.

"What is it?" she whispered. Even though the sun was up and getting higher in the sky, there were still shadows among the trees. Was a mountain lion stalking them? Or a bear?

"I thought I heard something," he said quietly.

She swallowed nervously and moved closer to him again. "Like…like a mountain lion?" She looked around them quickly, side to side, but saw no movement.

He stared at her for a moment and she watched as his expression changed from one of concern to amusement. He almost—*almost*—smiled.

"Angel."

She frowned. "What?"

"My name. It's Angel."

At that, she did smile. "Now was that so hard?"

He looked past her, his gaze going to where they'd come from. Was he looking for a mountain lion? Or perhaps he thought someone was chasing after them. She hoped it was the latter.

"Come on."

She followed after him again, keeping up with his long strides. "Are you going to tell me anything else?" She heard him sigh. "Like...where you're from," she prompted.

"From?"

"You know, I'm from Dallas," she said. "I'm assuming you're ex-military."

He laughed. "You deduced all of that, huh? You must be a detective."

"You're making fun of me," she stated.

"Yes."

After a little while, she said, "So...Angel is a nice name."

He laughed loudly but didn't comment.

She wondered why she was trying to make conversation with this man who held her hostage. Maybe it was simply her nervousness that kept her talking.

"My given name is Samantha, but everyone calls me Sam." She smiled. "Well, now they do. I used to hate it. But Tori, she... well, I think she called me Sam just to piss me off," she said. "I remember exactly what she said when we were first assigned as partners. She said, 'Do your friends call you Sam?'" Sam laughed slightly at the memory. "I told her 'not if they expect me to answer them.' But she called me Sam from that moment on." She paused. "Everyone calls me Sam now."

She assumed he would not comment on that either and she was surprised when he did.

"I'm sure your police department frowned on your personal relationship. Didn't they?"

"Well, yeah. But I was dating Robert at the time," she said. "He wanted to marry me."

He snorted. "So this Tori person...what? Converted you to the dark side?"

She nearly smiled as she recognized amusement in his voice. "Not converted," she said. "How about she showed me the light?" She tried to loosen the rope around her wrists where it rubbed against her skin. "It wasn't like it was instantaneous, you know. We became friends. I was...well, I was attracted to her and I wasn't really sure what to do about it."

He stopped again suddenly and stared behind them as he'd done earlier. She did the same.

"You know, you're really starting to scare me," she said.

He stared at her. "I'm just now starting? I must be losing my touch."

"What do you hear?"

"I'm not sure."

She again took a step closer to him. "Do mountain lions attack in the daylight?" she asked quietly.

"Not usually, no."

"Bears?"

He shook his head. "Bears will be the least of your worries," he said as he started walking again.

She kept quiet as she followed him. She knew what that remark was intended to mean.

CHAPTER EIGHT

"Are you sure she knows what she's doing?" Tori asked skeptically as Agent Ross crisscrossed back and forth in front of them. Her pack looked heavy, especially with a rifle strapped to the back of it, but Ross didn't seem hampered by the weight.

"She's making sure there's no false trail," Andrea said.

"I thought she'd already found the trail," she said as they followed behind. "Seems like we're wasting time."

"Agent Hunter, we'll be wasting time if we get off his mark and have to backtrack," Ross called from up ahead.

Tori glanced at Andrea and noted the amused expression on her face. "I don't think I like her," she said quietly.

"She grows on you," Andrea said.

Tori tried to curb her impatience as Agent Ross stopped and bent down, picking up a rock and studying it. She was very nearly tapping her foot at the delay. She wanted to bolt into the woods and start calling for Sam. She could almost feel the clock ticking.

"Shouldn't we have helicopters out?"

"No. Cameron says not yet."

"Why? That seems logical," she said.

Ross motioned for them to follow. *Finally*. Ross had her head down and Tori followed close behind. She had to admit, she had no clue as to what trail they were following. She could see nothing to indicate the area was disturbed.

"He would assume helicopters would be looking for him," Ross said.

"And?"

"And when they're not, it'll confuse him."

"Are we trying to goddamn confuse him or are we trying to rescue Sam?"

"Our mission is to rescue Samantha Kennedy," Ross said. She stopped and turned. "If there are no helicopters out, I'm hoping he slows his pace."

"If there are no helicopters out, he might decide he doesn't need a hostage after all," Tori said. "For Sam's sake, wouldn't it be better for him to think that we're on his trail?"

"It's a chance we have to take. He's got a good head start on us. If we have any hope of catching up to them, he's got to slow his pace. Angel Figueroa is an expert at this."

"I still think we should have an air search going on," she said.

"I'm well aware of what you think, Agent Hunter. But it's not your call. Even if we had a helicopter right on top of him, they'd never see him. I know this guy. He's a ghost."

Tori had to bite her lip to keep from replying. There didn't seem to be a sense of urgency in Agent Ross's actions. And Tori really, really needed urgency. She turned to Agent Sullivan, who gave her a slight shrug.

"Cameron, how far do you think they could have traveled last night?" Andrea asked.

Tori felt like the question was staged. Surely they had already discussed that.

"There was no moon so I would imagine he had to stop at full dark." Agent Ross looked directly at Tori. "And if we can stop discussing it and get on the move, perhaps we can make up some ground."

Tori narrowed her eyes. "Then lead on." Damn. *Arrogant… obnoxious.* She stepped aside, letting Andrea go first. The farther away she was from Cameron Ross, the better.

* * *

"Is it safe to drink?" Sam asked as he filled their water bottles at the stream.

"I wouldn't chance it without purification tablets," he said. "You worried about getting a little diarrhea?"

She nodded as she chewed the energy bar he'd given her. "Considering the limited bathroom options I have…yes."

As he'd been filling the water, she'd made scuff marks in the dirt where she sat. She'd dropped the wrapper to the energy bar behind the rock she sat on, hoping he didn't notice.

He sat down beside her and shook each water bottle several times. She assumed that was to dissolve the tablets. He was close to her and her eyes were drawn to the sheath—and the knife—strapped to his thigh. He followed her gaze, then shifted away from her.

"That knife will cut through flesh like soft butter," he said quietly with only a hint of a threat in his voice.

"I'm…I'm sure it can," she said. Although if she had to choose, she'd rather have a bullet to the head than have her throat cut. She mentally rolled her eyes at her morbid thought. Tori would find her before that. *Right?*

"So…Samantha, this partner of yours. You said you met at Dallas PD, yet you say she's FBI."

"Yes. And please, it's Sam," she said. "After Tori and I became…well, became involved, I transferred to CIU. That's Criminal Investigative Unit," she explained. "Tori and John became partners. John Sikes. They used to hate each other," she said with a smile, remembering their constant bickering. "Anyway, they had a horrible case. Identical twin brothers." She shook her head. "John almost died. He had his throat cut," she said as her eyes drifted to his knife again. "Tori, well, she had a really hard time with it and needed a change." She shrugged. "So FBI."

"And you think she's looking for you now?"

"Of course."

He shook his head. "We're not on a trail. We're bushwhacking. I don't think there's anyone following."

She met his gaze. "She's coming for me," she said with confidence.

His gaze went to the sky and he scanned overhead. "I am kinda wondering why we haven't had helicopters buzzing around though." He looked back at her. "Aren't you?"

She nodded. "Yes."

"Why do you think that is?"

She felt her heart sink. "They think we're in a vehicle. On the road."

His smile had a touch of smugness to it. "I imagine they have roadblocks set up in all directions."

Fear set in again. "Which means you don't really need me then."

He shrugged nonchalantly. "Oh, I'll keep you around for another day or so. They'll eventually figure out we're on foot. It'll be too late by then, of course."

Too late for her, in other words. She looked away from him, wondering how she could possibly escape. She was still tied to him. And even if she did run, he would most certainly catch her. Or shoot her in the back. Or a mountain lion would get her. God, she wished he'd never mentioned the damn mountain lion to begin with. Every twig that snapped in the woods she expected to see one about to attack them.

She watched as he pulled what appeared to be a map from his back pocket. He unfolded it and studied it for a bit, nodding ever so slightly. He folded it up neatly again and slipped it back into his pocket.

He stood then and pulled her up. "Time to move," he said.

She grimaced as the rope cut into the blisters on her wrist. She followed behind him, noticing that one of them had begun to bleed. Great. One more thing to attract a mountain lion.

They walked on without speaking, her following behind him. She wondered if she picked up a rock, could she use it to smash his skull? Could she knock him out long enough for her to escape? She had no clue as to where they were. Could she hide from him? Would Tori find her before he did? Or before a mountain lion did? She blew out her breath, feeling helpless. The silence between them wasn't helping. Sam couldn't stand it any longer.

"Angel? Can I ask you something?"

"I don't know. Can you?"

"Smart-ass," she murmured. "*May* I?" she clarified.

"Ask away. Can't promise I'll answer."

"Why are you running?" She paused. "I mean, I know you killed that girl. What else?" His pace slowed just a bit but still, she didn't think he was going to answer her.

"I killed…a lot of people." He stopped and glanced back at her. "That girl and her family being just four."

"Her family? You killed…a family?"

"I needed a distraction," he said as he continued on.

"From what?"

"Why do you want to know?"

"I told you, I'm a cop, I ask questions."

But he said no more, just continued on through the trees. They had been climbing again since they'd left the stream and she looked up, wondering how high they were. Her breathing was a bit labored. She chanced looking behind her, hoping… well, hoping someone—Tori—was coming for her. Instead, all she saw was trees and rocks, the yellowish hues of autumn turning the landscape a pretty golden color.

There was no sign of Tori.

CHAPTER NINE

"It's too early to stop," Agent Hunter said. "There's still daylight."

Cameron sighed and bit back her retort. She'd promised Andrea she would be nice. But really, Hunter was getting on her last nerve. As if *she* was the one doing the goddamn tracking.

"We've made good time," she said. "I don't want to ruin that by getting off his mark."

"You said Sam was leaving tracks," Hunter said. "We found the wrapper by the stream. We can keep—"

"We can't, Hunter. Okay? Will you just trust me?"

"We're wasting time, goddamn it!"

"Jesus Christ, we're not wasting time," she said loudly. "There are too many shadows." She tossed her backpack down with more force than was necessary. "We're tired. We're hungry. We'll pick up in the morning."

"I just think—"

"I don't care what you think," Cameron shot back.

Andrea raised her hands. "Will you two stop already? You're driving me insane with your constant arguing." She glared at Cameron. "Can we please try to get along?"

Cameron raised her eyebrows. Andrea was mad at *her*? No way. Hunter was the one being an ass about it. Hunter was the one who had questioned her every move all damn day. But the look in Andi's eyes told her not to argue. So she nodded, then flicked her glance to Hunter.

"I need to rest," she said. "It's mentally exhausting trying to follow their trail when there really isn't a trail."

Hunter nodded too. "Sorry. I guess I didn't think about it like that." She ran her hands through her short hair. "I'm just... I'm not used to feeling helpless like this."

"I'm sure you're not. And the only reason you're even on this trip is because Andrea told me to put myself in your shoes. So yeah, I'd have told Murdock to fuck himself and I'd have gone after her too."

She turned away and started gathering up firewood. She saw Andi doing the same. Hunter finally took off her backpack and tossed it to the ground as well.

"It feels good to get that off," Hunter said. "I'm not used to this. I'm a city girl."

"I was a city girl too," Andrea said. "Los Angeles. I moved to Sedona—that's in Arizona—and grew to love hiking." She looked at Cameron. "Cameron is the backpacker though. Military."

Hunter gave a quick laugh. "I should have known."

Cameron bristled. "What does that mean?"

"Bossy."

Andrea laughed too. "Oh, trust me. That's not the military talking."

Cameron looked at her. "What are you saying?"

"Oh, sweetheart, you know exactly what I'm saying."

Sweetheart? So Andi didn't feel the need to keep their relationship a secret? Hunter was FBI. And not that Murdock was oblivious, but it wasn't anything they talked about. Ever.

They didn't know Hunter. Certainly not enough to trust her with this. She looked at Andrea with a question in her eyes, and Andrea gave her the "don't be stupid" look. Yeah. They were sharing a tent. Hunter obviously knew they were more than just work partners.

Okay then.

* * *

"We'll stop here for the night," Angel said.

Sam glanced up, noting the sun was still streaking through the trees. As if reading her mind, he motioned to a cleared-out area with a previous fire ring.

"Flat ground. Not many rocks."

"Oh. That's good. Because I slept like crap last night." Then she smirked. "Not that I actually slept," she added. He looked at her blankly and she held her bound wrists up. "Uncomfortable." She didn't mention that sleeping next to him, with his gun and knife, was even more uncomfortable.

He pulled her arms up, his brow furrowed. "You're bleeding. Why didn't you say something?"

She shrugged. "You intend to kill me. I didn't think you'd be concerned with blisters on my wrists."

He met her eyes briefly, then quickly pulled his knife from its sheath. She took a step back, wondering if she'd said the wrong thing.

"For the rope," he explained.

So she held her arms out and he cut the rope from each wrist with surprising gentleness. She did note that the knife cut through the rope as if it were little more than thread. She immediately rubbed her wrists, then stretched her arms out to each side. She gave a satisfied moan as her muscles released some tension.

"I trust you won't do anything stupid?"

"I'm tired," she said. "And I'm really, really hungry. And please say there's something other than beef stew."

He laughed. "Yeah, I'll find something better." He pointed to a fallen pine limb. "Gather some wood for our fire. Once we get it going, I'll put something on your wound. I have a first-aid kit."

* * *

"So you live in a motorhome?" Tori asked as she stirred hot water into the pouch of mac and cheese. "That's your office?"

The question was addressed to Andrea, but it was Cameron who answered.

"She's a supercharged, custom-built motorhome," Cameron said. "It started out experimental. There is quite an impressive computer setup. I'd be dangerous if I really knew how to use it all."

"And your guy Murdock? He's the boss?"

"Murdock has three teams," Andrea said. "The other two are more conventional than us."

"But not as conventional as, say, your office," Cameron said. "We don't play by the same rules."

"I've heard about these teams that are made up of ex-military types," she said. "FBI's version of special ops?"

"A little, yes."

"So what kind of cases do you get?" she asked as she sampled the mac and cheese. It was decent. Not great.

"Mostly remote. Pretty much west of the continental divide. We had a serial killer in the California desert. We had a kidnapping in Idaho."

"There were the remains found in Nevada," Andrea said. "That ended up being from drug wars. And of course, the Patrick Doe case in Sedona."

Tori's head jerked up. "Patrick Doe? That was you?" She frowned. "Yeah, you called me. I thought your names sounded familiar."

"That was us," Cameron said. "That's where Andi and I met."

Tori nodded. "That's right. Andrea Sullivan. You were with the sheriff's department. I remember Casey saying you'd contacted her too." She arched one eyebrow. "So? That's where you met? And then you became...*colleagues*?"

Andrea laughed. "Yes. Colleagues."

"It's not advertised," Cameron said. "Murdock doesn't—"

"He knows," Andrea said. "Don't pretend he doesn't."

"Well, *he* pretends he doesn't," Cameron countered.

Tori smiled slightly. "When Sam and I first got together, Malone pretended he didn't know either. Malone was our lieutenant," she explained. "But Sam transferred to CIU, so we didn't have that issue."

Her smile faded completely. What was Sam doing right now? Was she cold? Hungry? Scared? How long before he didn't need her anymore?

"What do you know about this guy? Angel Figueroa."

Cameron shrugged. "We served together for a few of years. Same team."

"Doing what?"

Cameron met her gaze. "We were on a sniper team. Middle East, mostly. He got out a couple of years before I did," she said. "From what I heard, he didn't leave the Middle East or his profession. He's very good."

"Gun for hire?"

"Yeah."

"So what's he doing here? Murdock said everything was related, starting with a robbery in Santa Fe," Tori said.

"Yes, that's what he told us too. It was an armored car facility. Three million dollars." Cameron stuck another small limb on the fire. "Doesn't sound like the Angel I knew, but who knows? People change."

"But he's a killer?"

Cameron nodded. "Yes. He's a killer."

They were silent for a moment, then Andrea leaned closer. "I'll trade you some of this chicken stuff for some of your mac and cheese."

CHAPTER TEN

Sam savored the strong black coffee with a sigh. She'd slept better but not much. He'd left her hands untied, but the ground was hard and she'd gotten cold. And, of course, she was sharing the tent with a man and his gun. And a knife.

She looked at him from across the fire. "You didn't take the time for coffee yesterday," she stated. "You're not afraid of someone catching us?"

He lifted one corner of his mouth in a smile. "You still think someone is coming after you?"

"Yes."

He nodded as he folded up the map he'd been studying. "Yes, I suppose eventually they'll attempt to track us, once their roadblocks don't pan out. I can't imagine there'd be much of a trail by then." He motioned to her food. "How was it?"

Sam looked down at the pile of yellowish goo. Powdered eggs. "It was delicious," she said dryly.

He laughed. "Yes, I know." He held his hand out. "Give it here if you're not going to finish it."

"Chicken *stuff*?" Tori looked at her pouch, not really hungry anymore, but she nodded.

"I think we made good time today," Cameron said as if to ease her mind. "Another two days, we might get close."

"Two days?" Tori felt her spirits sink. Did Sam have two days?

She handed him what was left of her breakfast and he finished it off in three bites. She knew he would be ready to head out soon so she drank the last of her coffee.

"If we make good time, we'll camp by a river tonight," he said.

Her eyes lit up. "Like, a bath?" she asked hopefully.

"For you or me?"

She wrinkled up her nose. "Both."

He laughed again, and she thought he sure seemed to be in a good mood this morning. But at least he was talking about their next camp. That meant he wasn't getting ready to ditch her just yet. He stood and she was about to do the same when he sat back down again.

"Can I ask you something?"

She gave him a quick smile. "I don't know. *Can* you?"

He smiled too, then his expression turned serious. "The other night…the first night in the tent, you had this terrified look on your face."

She bit her lower lip. "Yes. I guess I did."

"You were afraid I was going to…"

"Yes."

"Had you been raped before?"

She was surprised at the gentleness of his question, by the genuine concern in his eyes. She nodded. "Yes."

"I'm sorry."

She shrugged. "It was…it was right before Tori and I…well, we weren't lovers yet," she said shyly. "We worked in Homicide and we were on a stakeout. We saw a drug deal go down, and well, we became targets. Anyway, we were leaving Tori's boat one evening and these guys grabbed me. They knocked Tori out and handcuffed her and threw her in the lake." She paused. "I thought she was dead," she said in a quiet voice. "They took me to this warehouse. Stripped me naked and tied me to a bed." Her hand was trembling. She set the cup down and linked her fingers together. "There were five of them in the room. They were taking turns." She closed her eyes. It was something she'd not thought about in a long time. "One guy had a whip and when he came toward me, I started screaming." She met his eyes. "Tori found me. She knocked down the door and started shooting. It was all so fast. I didn't have time to think. Tori was there. They were dead."

"I guess she survived the lake then."

Sam nodded and smiled. "Yes."

"I may be a lot of things, Sam, but I'm no rapist."

"I know. You would have already done it if you were."

* * *

Cameron had called for a rest and Tori had to hide her impatience. They'd only been at it for a few hours. But as Cameron had implied yesterday evening, she was the one doing all the work. Tori and Andrea were only following her.

She took off her backpack like they did and stretched her shoulders. The morning coolness was all but gone and she'd shed her sweatshirt an hour earlier. It was a sunny, cloudless day, making her long for shorts instead of jeans. But that would be foolish. As Cameron had explained, they were bushwhacking. They weren't on a trail.

They were stopped on a ledge, and she took that opportunity to look around. To really look around for the first time. Her eyes widened as she looked across the mountain and saw nothing but trees and woods and rocks for miles and miles. Not a single structure to be found.

"Damn. We're like in the middle of nowhere."

"I know exactly where we are," Cameron said with her normal arrogance.

"Of course you do," Tori mumbled as her gaze took in the view around her. It really was pretty up here. They'd only done a couple of hikes and most were near the campground and not strenuous. She could almost see the lure of a long backpacking trip. Almost. At the end of her hike though, she was ready for a cold beer. And a lawn chair chat with Casey while Sam and

Leslie got things ready for dinner. She smiled quickly as she pictured it, knowing how much she and Casey acted like typical guys. Sam and Leslie had said as much on several occasions.

"Here."

She turned as Cameron walked over to her. She had a gadget from her backpack and she touched the screen.

"GPS. Here's our location." Cameron tapped again. "This is the route we've taken so far." She made the image bigger. "Here's your campground."

"We've come a long way."

"Yeah. And as you can tell, he's not following the terrain at all. He goes up, then crosses over for a bit, then back up. He's definitely hiking as if someone is tracking him."

"And you're sure you're on his trail?"

Cameron turned off the device and returned it to her backpack, not bothering to answer the question. Tori turned to Andrea who gave her a quick smile.

"The problem is, you two are too much alike," Andrea said.

Tori nearly snorted. "I am *nothing* like her."

* * *

Sam walked gingerly behind him. They were on a ledge and she was afraid to look down. The drop looked…well, it looked like it would hurt if she fell. He'd left her hands untied again, and she wondered why she was being so amicable and not trying to escape. But then, where would she go? He was bigger and stronger and most likely ran much faster than she did. Of course, there was his threat that still haunted her. He would kill her when he didn't need her any longer. She supposed that wasn't really a threat. More like a matter-of-fact statement.

She pushed that thought aside and set her sights on the view around her. It was certainly beautiful up here and if the circumstances were different, she would be admiring the scenery and taking mental pictures, if not real ones. The air was fresher than she could ever remember it smelling, but she was also aware of her labored breathing as they climbed higher. Lost in thought and not paying attention, she felt her right foot start to slip. It was almost in slow motion that she felt herself falling.

"Angel!"

She reached out for him, just missing as her feet slipped away. She grabbed at rocks and the lone scrub brush that clung haphazardly to the ledge. She missed the brush and slipped farther down away from him.

"Sam!"

She felt a strong grip on her wrist, and she looked up, meeting his eyes. He was lying flat on his stomach, reaching over the edge for her.

"Hang on," he said. "I've got you."

With her free hand, she dug her fingers into the crevice of a rock, using all her strength to hold on. He slowly pulled her up and she reached out, clutching her hand tightly around his arm as she climbed the last few feet to the top.

She was breathing hard, her heart still pounding in her chest. She sat up and crawled away from the edge, still holding tight to his arm.

"Oh my God," she said between breaths. "I thought, well…"

He shook his head. "My fault. This was a stupid route to take."

She leaned forward just a tad, chancing a peek over the side. It wasn't quite as steep as she'd feared. She had at least ten or fifteen more feet before the bottom dropped off. *Damn.*

"Thank you," she said, finally releasing his arm. "I have just a…a tiny fear of heights."

"Now you tell me," he said with a smile. He stood up and held his hand out to her. "Come on. We've got to backtrack a bit. It's actually shorter."

"Shorter? To the river and my bath?"

"Yeah."

"Then why this?" she asked, motioning around them.

"In case we're being followed."

"Oh."

* * *

"Here's where they camped last night," Cameron said, pointing to the fire ring. She knelt down beside it and felt the ash. It was cold but powdery. Fresh.

"So we're not really making good time then," Tori said.

"No." Cameron looked to the sky, seeing white, puffy clouds gathering. They didn't look like rain clouds, but if they lingered through the day, they would block out the sun, bringing dusk to the mountainside earlier than normal. She glanced at Andrea. "How are you doing?"

Andi nodded. "I'm good."

Cameron nodded too. She felt like they hadn't had a second alone, which they hadn't. Last night in the tent, she'd been exhausted and had managed little more than a kiss before falling asleep. She was used to them working alone. Used to talking—saying—what she pleased. Used to their teasing, used to their playfulness. But playfulness and teasing had no place here, not with Hunter along. Not when her lover was the victim they were chasing.

And she didn't want to tell Hunter this, but Angel Figueroa was a cold-blooded killer, nothing more, nothing less than that. She'd seen him pull the trigger too many times. He was good at his job. Her only solace for Hunter was that they were still following two sets of tracks. How much time Sam Kennedy had left was anyone's guess though.

She tightened the straps on her backpack and headed out again. It looked like they were heading up the side of the mountain. She got her GPS out and studied the terrain. If her guess was right, they'd be hard-pressed to find a place to make camp. That was probably why Angel had camped here, where it was still flat. Well, they had no choice but to push on. She guessed they were at least three hours behind him, if not more.

"Looks like we're climbing, ladies," she said as she took off.

CHAPTER ELEVEN

Sam stood transfixed as the crystal clear water splashed across the rocks. She imagined it was cold, but she didn't care. She was hot and sweaty and wanted nothing more than a bath and to wash her hair.

She turned, looking behind her toward their camp. Angel had put the tent up thirty or forty feet from the river. They appeared to be lower again in elevation as there were only a handful of pines. Most of the trees were the fragrant junipers. Angel was busy gathering firewood and the sound of the gurgling water beckoned her. He'd said he'd give her privacy and she believed him. So she walked a little farther away to where a shallow pool was. It looked inviting. Cold, but inviting. She listened to the sound of the rushing water, then heard other sounds that she'd not taken the time to notice before: birds calling and the wind as it rustled the lone pine near her. It was nice. It was relaxing. She looked over once again and Angel had his back to her.

"No sense in being modest," she murmured.

She kicked her boots off, then pushed her jeans and underwear down in one motion. She had a flannel shirt over her T-shirt. She'd stripped off Tori's sweatshirt that morning and tied it around her waist. She paused to smell the T-shirt and wrinkled her nose.

She decided to rinse it out. It might not be dry by morning but at least it would be cleaner. The tiny bar of soap Angel had given her was clutched in her hand as she took a step into the water.

"*Jesus*," she hissed as the cold penetrated all the way to her bones.

She reminded herself that she didn't care how cold it was. She walked in, past her knees, then nearly to her waist. That was as deep as the pool was. She silently counted to three, then sunk down over her head. She stood up quickly, shivering. But she ignored the cold. She lathered the soap and washed herself, feeling better already. She dipped under again, wetting her hair thoroughly before rubbing soap in it. It wasn't the silky smooth shampoo she was used to but it did the job.

She was absolutely freezing when she got out and she used her shirt to dry herself a little before putting her jeans back on. She felt ten times better. Cold, but better.

When she made her way back to camp, Angel was nowhere to be found. She had a moment of panic as she looked around her.

"Angel?" she called. "Angel?"

Had he left her? But no, his pack was there. The tent was already assembled. Then she heard movement and turned, finding him walking along the stream from the opposite direction as she'd been. Apparently he'd taken his own bath.

"Feel better?"

She nodded. "Much."

"Me too."

She relaxed again, although that thought struck her as odd. She was more relaxed in her captor's presence than not. Well, there was the threat of mountain lions.

She motioned to the water. "You think there might be trout in there?"

"I imagine so."

"Doesn't that sound...you know, good for dinner?"

He raised his eyebrows. "You want to go fishing?"

"Well, I was thinking maybe you would," she said, smiling slightly. "Fresh fish sounds so much better than one of those things you've got there," she said, pointing to his pack. She wiped the smile from her face, realizing how that sounded. He could be starving her if he wanted to. "Not that I'm complaining," she added quickly. Then, "Much." He actually laughed and she relaxed again. "Is that a yes?"

"I guess I could try. I'll have to improvise. I don't carry fishing gear," he said.

"Maybe on your next trip, you should add that to your list."

He was smiling as he rummaged through his pack. She smiled too, but she was feeling blue. Fishing made her think of Tori. Talking about Tori made her feel better.

"I don't really like to fish," she said. He looked up but said nothing. "Tori loves it. We have this boat. It's a cabin cruiser. She keeps it on Eagle Mountain Lake, just west of Fort Worth," she said. "Casey and Tori go fishing. Leslie and I talk and read and sit in the sun." She paused. "And bring them a cold beer on request." She sighed, wondering if she would ever get to do that again. "Usually on the days we plan to cook the fish they caught, they don't catch anything," she said with a quick laugh. She met his gaze when he looked at her again. "I'm sorry," she said quickly. "I miss her."

He nodded and held up a piece of wire. "I can bend it into a hook."

"What will we use for line?"

"More importantly, what will we use for bait?"

"Oh." She hadn't even thought of that.

Angel tossed her the rope. "Untwist the twine," he said. "I'll see if I can find something."

She started on her task while keeping an eye on him. He went to a fallen tree and started pulling off the bark. After a few minutes, he held up what appeared to be a beetle of some sort. He walked back over, looking skeptically at her.

"Not sure it'll work," he said.

She watched silently as he made a loop with the wire then tied the twine to it. About a foot higher, he made a knot in the twine and secured a small rock.

"For weight," he said to her unasked question.

He made a crude hook, then unceremoniously impaled the unlucky beetle. Without being asked, she followed him to the stream. He walked downstream a bit, then tossed the twine in the water upstream. The water carried it downstream past them and he pulled it out. The beetle was gone.

"There's more where that came from."

He handed her the fishing twine, and he nearly jogged back to the fallen tree. He brought another beetle with him and repeated the impaling process. This time, he bent the wire a bit at the tip. Again, he tossed it in the stream, letting it float down. This time, the beetle was still on there. He repeated this several times before he got a hit. He jerked the line out of the water and Sam's eyes widened as a trout came out with it. Disappointment quickly followed as the fish twisted off the make-do hook and landed safely back in the water. Unfortunately, the beetle was gone.

"Damn, that was close," she said excitedly. "Is it bad for me to say that I could almost taste him?"

"Well, we better catch one. Now you've got me salivating for fresh trout too."

After a third beetle was sacrificed, the line was once again tossed into the stream. Sam stood nearby, hands rubbing together in anticipation. On his fourth try, a trout hit and he jerked the line hard. Sam saw the twine go taut, then a trout jumped out of the water much like the first one. This one, though, did not twist free.

"You got one, you got one!" she said, clapping her hands.

"He's not on shore yet," Angel warned as he backed away from the water, pulling the twine with him.

Finally, the fish was securely out of the water and it was a nice big one. Sam felt sorry for it as it flipped back and forth on the rocky shore. But only for a moment. All she had to do was remember the meals she'd had the last two nights.

Angel held him up, offering him to Sam. Sam held up her hands and shook her head as she took a step backward.

"Oh, no. No, no," she said. "I don't actually *clean* them," she said. "I *cook* them."

"But I caught him," Angel said. "Seems fair that you should clean him."

Sam grinned. "That logic doesn't work for Tori, it's certainly not going to work for you." Then she laughed. "Of course, if you want to give me your knife…"

"No. On second thought, I should probably clean him."

"Thought that would be your answer." She glanced over to their campsite. "So, you do have something to cook him in, right?"

He motioned to his pack with a toss of his head. "There's some cooking gear. Not much. Help yourself."

As she sorted through the stuff in his pack, it occurred to her that they were not exactly acting like hostage and captor. Had they really ever? Of course, for her, that was a good thing. She'd taken enough psychology classes, had sat through enough training seminars on hostage situations to know that the more the abductor thought of the hostage as a person and not a prisoner, the better the chance for a positive outcome.

She turned her head, watching for a moment as he knelt by the stream, cleaning the fish. It would be a lot less stressful if she thought of this as a backpacking trip and not a forced march on the mountain with a killer. But then, there was the girl. Sam could still see her bloody face, her stained clothes. She could still see Leslie lying on the ground from a wound he inflicted. She closed her eyes for a moment and shook those thoughts away. He was Angel and she was Sam, and she was going to cook them dinner.

"Find what you need?"

"I think…I think I can use this," she said, holding up a small pan. She looked at the trout he held. It wouldn't fit.

As if reading her mind, he said, "I can cut it up."

"Okay. That'll work." She moved other stuff around in his pack. "Seasonings?" she asked hopefully. "And a side dish?"

"A side dish?"

"Something with rice or potatoes?"

"Yeah, there's some instant mashed potatoes," he said.

She smiled. "Then we'll practically have a feast."

* * *

"This is where we'll sleep?" Tori looked around at the slope. "On the side of a goddamn mountain?"

"You were the one who wanted to push on," Cameron reminded her.

That was true. Tori blew out her breath as she let her pack fall to the ground. Andrea was already collecting firewood. Cameron was assembling their tent. Yeah, *their* tent. Tori looked at her pack, then untied her own tent. God, what she wouldn't give to have Sam with her right now. She'd been able to push her loneliness away for the most part. She was a part of the rescue mission, that was the important thing. Only this *rescue* mission wasn't like anything she'd been a part of before. Cameron Ross was calling the shots and her sense of urgency was lacking, in Tori's opinion. But hell, they *were* in the middle of goddamn nowhere.

On the side of a mountain.

She shook out her tent and went about assembling it. They were on a rocky slope, and she moved as many rocks out of the way as she could. Cameron had taken their tent into the woods although the slope seemed even more drastic there than on the edge. Well, maybe they wanted privacy.

"If we don't come to a stream soon, we're going to be in trouble," Andrea said as she shook her water bottle. "I have one more full one. How are you two?"

"Yeah, me too," Cameron said. "Enough for dinner and coffee."

Great.

"But we'll find water," Cameron said. "Angel's in the same situation we are."

Tori was too tired to comment. She walked over to the fire ring Andrea had assembled, then glanced around, looking for downed wood to add to the pile. She walked alone into the woods, picking up small limbs as she went. Loneliness settled on her shoulders, and she tried to shake it off. It was almost surreal—this trek through the woods that she'd been on. One minute they'd been resting comfortably at the RV, enjoying the evening. If Casey had ever gotten a fire going, they'd have sat around it while dinner was cooking. They'd have beer. Or wine. Most likely Sam and Leslie would have brought out a bottle of wine and she and Casey would have pretended to enjoy it more than the beer. Then they would have wanted something with a bit more substance…like that nice bottle of scotch she'd brought.

But no. They'd answered the call. Like they were trained to do. When someone was in distress, you went. No questions asked. And she and Casey had gone. And now Sam was missing. Abducted by the same man who'd killed that family, the same man who had taken three million dollars, the same man who had killed his accomplices.

And that same man had Sam.

And she couldn't do a goddamn thing about it.

CHAPTER TWELVE

Andrea shifted again, trying to get comfortable. It had been an awful night's sleep. She swore there was a rock the size of a softball under her back. She lifted her arm out of the sleeping bag and touched her watch, illuminating the face. Thank God. It was nearly time to get up. She rolled over closer to Cameron and snaked her arm around her waist. Cameron appeared to still be sleeping soundly and didn't wake.

Andrea had to admit that she missed the motorhome, missed Lola. She missed their normal routine when on a case. Because even then, at the end of the day, they went home to their bed, their kitchen, their *life*. Here? No. Nothing about this was familiar. For Cameron, maybe so. She'd done this type of thing for years in the military. But Andrea missed taking a shower, missed having hot coffee in the morning, missed cooking them breakfast. And she missed having a bathroom.

"What are you thinking about?" Cameron whispered.

"I thought you were sleeping."

Cameron rolled toward her. "Who could sleep? God, I miss our bed." She leaned closer and kissed Andrea gently.

"I miss our shower."

"Yeah. I miss Lola."

Andrea laughed quietly. "I know. I hope she's okay."

"I threatened to kill him if anything happened to her. I'm sure she's fine."

"You did?"

"Yeah. Right after I threatened to kill him if he wrecked the rig or touched the computers." Cameron sat up and rubbed her face. "And I miss our shower too."

"At least we have toiletries. I keep thinking about Samantha. Has he given her anything? I mean, is he even feeding her?"

"If he wants her to hike and keep up with him, he is."

"You know him," she said. "Does she have a chance?" It was too dark to see Cameron's expression, but she could imagine it.

"He's a bastard, that's for sure," Cameron said. "One of the requirements to being a sniper is to not show remorse after a kill. And I never once saw him show any emotion."

"I wish we could offer Tori some hope."

"I wish we could too." Cameron tossed off her sleeping bag. "Let's try to get an early start. Since we're on the ledge like this, we'll get the morning light. That should give us an extra half hour, at least." She paused. "I'm going to call Murdock."

Andrea finally sat up, knowing it was time to start the day. Cameron had already unzipped their tent and was putting on her boots. She heard rustling outside and assumed Tori was up too. Each morning so far, Tori had been up and waiting for them. Andrea felt a twinge of guilt each time too, but knew they had to wait on the sun before starting out.

She let out a heavy sigh. "God, I miss my shower."

But she put her boots on too, noting that her feet were a little sore. As she stood up, she realized that her back was sore too. And her shoulders. Guess she wasn't in as good of shape as she thought.

Tori already had the fire going, and she walked up to it, holding her hands out to its warmth.

"Good morning," she said. "How did you sleep?"

"Probably about as well as you did."

"Rocks under your back too?"

"Rocks and a damn tree root."

Andrea looked around. "Where's Cameron?"

Tori motioned with her head. "She headed up the trail. Had a flashlight out."

"She said she was going to call Murdock," Andrea said. "I guess to check in and give him our GPS coordinates."

Hunter was quiet for a moment, then looked up at her. "Can I ask you something?"

"Of course."

"How did you get her to let me come along?"

Andrea smiled. "I told her if I was the one who had been taken hostage, I hoped that she would not let anyone stand in her way when it came to finding me."

Tori nodded. "Thank you." She looked down at the fire. "I just keep thinking we're going too slow." She looked up again. "And I keep thinking…if something happens to Sam, I'm not going to make it out of here with my sanity. Like I said, she's my whole life." Tori shook her head. "Before I met her, I was… well, I wasn't a very nice person. And I didn't have anybody in my life. No friends." She shrugged. "Even the job, I wasn't in any kind of a relationship with anyone. I did my job, that's all. And everyone tolerated me, I guess. Then Sam came along and I…God, she was dating this guy. Robert." Tori smiled. "What a jerk he was."

"You said you and Sam were partners on the force?"

Tori nodded. "Yeah. Homicide. Me and partners, well, I'd gone through a few of them. Like I said, I wasn't a very nice person. But Sam, she didn't take any shit from me. And we had so much happen to us, we just got so close. And the attraction was there for both of us. Of course, she had Robert to deal with. He wanted to marry her." Tori stirred the fire a bit. "I fell in love with her and I was afraid to tell her." She looked up with a smile. "She, of course, was having the same problem."

"I imagine it was hard having a man in the picture," she said.

"You have no idea." Tori stared at her. "Or do you?"

Andrea laughed. "God, no. I knew I was gay when I was in high school."

Tori nodded. "Yeah. I knew at a young age too. But Sam…" Tori smiled. "Well, she likes to say she's a late bloomer."

"When did you go to the FBI?" she asked.

Tori looked up at her. "After the Patrick Doe case, actually. My partner, John Sikes, he nearly lost his life. It was a bad case all around. We thought we had the bastard and it ended up being his twin."

"Yes, I remember your notes on it."

"I needed…a change," Tori said.

Andrea turned when she heard Cameron coming back down the trail. The sky was lightening up quickly, and she assumed they would head out soon.

"I asked Murdock to send out a helicopter this morning," Cameron said. "If we don't send one out, Angel is bound to think it odd."

"I thought you wanted to confuse him," Tori said.

"Yeah. That's why I'm sending one out now. Only not too close. Close enough for Angel to hear it, but far enough away for him to think we don't know where he is."

"But why not—"

Cameron held up her hand. "I'm not arguing about this with you, Hunter. We're not using the helicopter to spot them. It's our job to find them."

Andrea was surprised that Tori seemed to accept that statement and didn't protest further. Cameron seemed surprised as well.

"Let's break camp," Cameron said. "There'll be enough light soon. We can pick up their trail again."

CHAPTER THIRTEEN

"So how did you get your name?" Sam asked. They were traveling on even ground and didn't seem to be climbing at all. The forest was a little thicker here than in the last two days. She found the hiking easy this morning. Easy enough to talk and not be out of breath.

"You mean since I'm a killer?"

"Well, your mother must have thought you were special. She gave you such a beautiful name."

Angel stopped suddenly but didn't turn around. Sam wondered if bringing up his mother was taboo.

"My mother was the angel," he finally said. He turned to look at her then. "She died," he said without much emotion.

"I'm sorry," Sam said immediately. His eyes had a faraway look, and she knew he was remembering her.

"I…I was sixteen. And I have yet to forgive my father."

"He…he killed her?" she asked quietly.

Angel nodded. "A car accident. He'd been drinking. He was always drinking. He took a corner too fast. Swerved to miss another car and ended up flipping them over. He walked away without a scratch."

Sam instinctively reached out and squeezed his arm. "I'm so sorry. Did you have siblings to turn to?"

"No. And the son of a bitch didn't even do jail time. I left home, went to live with the family of a friend. When I turned eighteen, I joined the military."

She wanted to ask a hundred more questions, but she held back. She let him reminisce without her pestering him with questions. After a few seconds, he nodded and she let her hand slip from his arm. He started walking again and she followed. But of course her curiosity got the best of her. She waited what she thought was an acceptable amount of time before asking her next question.

"So the military? What did you do?"

He laughed. "Do you really want to know?"

"Do I *not* want to know?" she countered.

"I ended up in a Special Ops unit," he said.

"Okay. That means what?"

"My team was made up of sharpshooters." He stopped again and turned to her. "I was a sniper. I assassinated people."

"Oh. I see."

"Yeah. That's where I got my start. You're trained to kill without thinking about it. It became too easy," he said. "And I was very, very good at it."

Okay, so this conversation is going downhill fast.

"What else do you want to know?" he asked.

She met his gaze. "That's probably more than enough."

"Thought it'd be."

* * *

"What the hell?"

"What is it?" Andrea asked.

"I got two trails here."

"What do you mean?" Hunter asked as she walked up beside her.

Cameron pointed up the hill. "They go up here. This is what we've been following." Then she pointed to the left, into the woods. "But I've got a broken limb on this scrub brush. See the indention where this rock has been moved?" She stood up. "So the trail goes this way."

"Maybe it's from other hikers," Andrea suggested.

"No. It's them." Cameron squinted into the sun as she looked up the ridge. *What the hell was he doing?* "Backtracking?"

"What?"

She shook her head. "Thinking out loud." She walked up the trail a few steps then turned back. "It's very steep. I can't believe he'd take this route." She motioned to Andi. "Andrea, please stay there." Andrea nodded. "Hunter, come with me."

"Sam's not crazy about heights," Tori said as she looked over the edge. "And right now, I'm not either."

"See the rocks dislodged. They definitely came up this way." Cameron hurried up, knowing in her gut that they'd backtracked. Maybe he'd gone up here for show. Maybe he wanted to confuse them. Hell, maybe it got too steep and they had to turn around. She felt like they were wasting precious time, but she had to be sure.

She stopped when she saw the skid marks off to the side, the smooth dirt where a body had been dragged. *Christ, did she go over the side?* Cameron looked down, seeing where the skid stopped.

"Look here," she said.

"What does that mean?" Hunter squatted down. "Looks like someone slipped here."

"Yeah. That someone is your Sam."

Hunter looked up at her. "What are you saying? She fell off the goddamn side?" Hunter stood back up, peering over the side much like Cameron had done.

"No, no. It's not like it's a sheer drop off. She would have only slid down twenty feet or so. But no, the marks stop there," she said, pointing. She walked up the trail a little more but found no evidence that they'd continued. "My guess is, this was steeper than he thought. Not only was it slowing them down, Sam being an inexperienced hiker proved to be a liability."

"So they went back down and took an easier route."

"Exactly. But route to where?" Cameron pulled out her GPS, intending to look at the new route into the forest. "If I had access to my computers in the rig, I could put our daily coordinates into one of the algorithms Jason wrote for me. We could at least get a probability of his intended target."

Hunter stared at her. "You can do that? So why don't you, like, remote in or something."

"Yeah, if it were only that easy." She held up the device. "This is all I got. No computer."

"Can't you call it in? Have someone else do it?"

"Who? One of the rangers? The sheriff's deputies?"

"Murdock?"

"Yeah. I could do that. When we stop tonight, I'll compile our coordinates. If I've got a strong enough signal, I'll email it to him. Maybe he can get Jason on it."

She studied the terrain, trying to see where he might be heading. This route, along the ridge, looped back down to the other side. If they are now traveling around it, while still going slightly up, they'd end up...where?

"There's a river," she said. "He's probably carrying less water than we are. He'd need to refill." She looked at Hunter. "I'm guessing that's where they made camp. Sound plausible?"

Hunter nodded. "Works for me."

"Yeah. Let's go." She headed back down to where they'd left Andrea.

"So who is Jason? Is he on your team?"

"My team is Andrea. No, Jason is at Quantico. Computer geek. He designed my setup in the rig and the truck. He wrote all of the programs I use." She grinned. "Like I said, I'd really be dangerous if I knew how to use them all."

Andrea was waiting where they'd left her, and she raised her eyebrows questioningly. "They went this way, right?"

"You turning into a tracker?"

Andrea smiled at her. "Yeah. Because this way looks a lot easier."

"Yeah. We found where they stopped. Looks like Sam may have stumbled and gone off the side a bit."

"What? Like fell?"

"No, just slid a little," Tori said. "Maybe she did it on purpose, trying to slow him down."

"Could have," Cameron said. "She's been doing great by leaving marks behind. Like breaking this limb here." She headed into the woods. "Let's see if we can't make up some time on them." She paused, her eyes going to the sky. "Listen," she said.

"What? I don't hear anything," Hunter said.

"Wait for it."

Maybe it was her military training, but she'd recognize the distant low rumble of a helicopter anywhere.

Andrea was the first to hear it. "Helicopter."

"I hear it now," Tori said.

"Let's hope Angel can hear it too."

* * *

Sam tilted her head, listening. Angel stopped, doing the same. He turned to her.

"Looks like they finally gave up on finding us with a roadblock," he said.

"They don't sound like they're very close," she said.

"Probably doing a perimeter search around the campground in all directions," he said. He started hiking again. "If that's the case, they probably won't get up this far until tomorrow."

Sam hurried to catch up with him. "You don't sound worried," she said.

"I can hide from a helicopter." He glanced back at her as he kept walking. "As long as you don't do anything stupid."

"Have I done anything stupid so far?"

"No. You've been a model hostage," he said with amusement in his voice. "Why is it that you haven't tried to escape?"

"Where would I go? I mean, say I could outrun you because, well, maybe you trip on a rock and knock yourself out," she said with a quick laugh. "So I get away. Then what? I don't know where I am. I have no food or water. I have no tent."

"True."

"And then there's the fear of a mountain lion. Thank you for putting *that* seed in my head," she said.

"So you've accepted your fate, huh?" He looked back at her again. "Or are you still holding out hope that you'll get rescued?"

"Yes. Tori is coming for me. I know it." And she did. It was more than wishful thinking. She could almost *feel* her coming.

"I admire your faith," Angel said.

"It's easy. She loves me. She would do anything in her power to find me." When he didn't say anything, she decided to probe. "You ever been in love, Angel?"

He paused only a moment, then answered her with a very curt no.

CHAPTER FOURTEEN

Andrea splashed water on her face at the river, letting out a satisfied groan. She was hot and sweaty, and it felt oh so good.

"Wish we had time for a bath," she said longingly.

"Sorry," Cameron said. She bent down next to the fire ring and felt the ash. "They camped here last night. We're making better time."

"How far ahead are they?" Tori asked.

"I'd guess a few hours still," Cameron said evasively. She walked over to the stream too and knelt down, splashing her face much as Andrea had done. "I don't think we'll catch up tomorrow though."

"We've still got most of the day left," Tori said.

"So do they," Cameron said. "When you fill your water bottles, don't forget to add the purification tablets."

Andrea ran her wet hands through her hair, then pulled it back in a ponytail and slipped it through the back of her cap. She was aware of Cameron watching her.

"I think I'm going to get my hair cut," she said, wondering what Cameron's reaction would be.

Cameron glanced at her, then slid her gaze to Tori before looking back with raised eyebrows. "Oh? Why?"

Andrea shrugged. "I'm hot and sweaty, and I don't like it on my neck. It would be something different. And I wouldn't have to do this to get it out of my face."

"But if you cut it off, you won't be able to do that."

Andrea tilted her head and frowned. "Right. That's my point."

"But…" Cameron looked again at Tori and turned slightly, giving them a little privacy. "Andi? Like cut it short? No."

"No? Why not? Yours is short." She looked around Cameron to Tori. "Tori's is short."

"First of all, mine is not that short. You're the one always reminding me that I need a cut," Cameron said as she ran her fingers through her sandy hair. "Now Hunter here, that's short. Please say not like that."

Andrea very nearly rolled her eyes.

"Sam wears hers shorter now too," Tori said from behind them. "Not that it was ever really long. About like yours." She paused. "It was like blond silk. And when she asked my opinion on getting it cut, I told her no way." Tori smiled. "She cut it that same day." She shrugged. "And I love it now."

Andrea nodded. "Yeah. I think I'm going to get it cut."

Cameron threw up her hands. "Whatever. Cut off your beautiful hair if you want to. It's your hair."

Tori laughed. "Yeah, I think that's the line I used too."

Andrea smiled and shook her head as she filled up her water bottles like the others were doing. Cameron had already scoped out the area and determined that they did not cross the river. Of course, that didn't mean that they didn't cross it later on.

They walked single file again, with Tori between them this time. Andrea knew Tori was worried about Sam, but she'd done a good job of hiding it. Even her bickering with Cameron had lessened. Or Cameron's bickering with her. They were both strong-willed and thought they were right. Andrea had learned how to temper Cameron's stubbornness. She wondered if Sam could control Tori with just a look too.

She tried to imagine what Sam Kennedy was like. Tori's affection for her was deep, obviously. Andrea imagined her to be soft where Tori was hard. She imagined Sam was a people person, making up for Tori's rather gruff demeanor. Of course, Tori's behavior in this situation might not be anything like who she really was. Stressful situations usually exposed all sides of a person.

While their pace was quick, Cameron had to stop a few times to get her bearings. At one point, she lost the trail under a canopy of thick trees. They were walking on nothing but pine needles and nothing looked disturbed. Andrea and Tori waited while Cameron crisscrossed the area, finally finding a mark Sam must have left.

"Here."

Andrea walked closer. It was but a small indention in the earth, and she wondered how Cameron had even spotted it.

"Are you sure?"

Cameron paused. "No. Son of a bitch," she muttered. "Stay here. Both of you."

Andrea nodded, and she looked at Tori who was watching Cameron intently. Cameron went back to where they'd lost the trail and backtracked a bit, then got back on it. She walked carefully, perhaps putting her feet where she thought Angel and Sam had walked. When she got to the bed of pine needles, she stopped.

"What's she doing?" Tori whispered.

"Because of the ground cover, Angel might have used that as an opportunity to take a sharp turn," she said. She looked at Tori. "She'll find the trail. Don't worry."

Tori nodded, but her eyes remained glued to Cameron.

Cameron looked up. "Andi, come here."

Andrea nodded and joined her.

"Keep on my mark."

Andrea stood where Cameron had been, then watched as Cameron went left and right, ten spaces out, then back. She repeated this three times before she found their trail again. It was nearly twenty-five feet from where Andrea stood.

"Got it." Cameron pointed to a broken tip on the limb of a young pine. "She's doing good."

Before they'd gone ten steps, however, a single gunshot—far off in the distance—broke the silence. She and Cameron exchanged glances.

Tori tilted her head. "Did you hear that?"

"Yeah. It could be anyone."

Andrea could see the panic in Tori's eyes.

"It could be Sam," Tori said as she headed up the hill.

Cameron grabbed her arm and pulled her to a stop.

"What the hell do you think you're doing?"

"That could be Sam!" Tori yelled, yanking her arm out of Cameron's grasp.

"It could be anybody," Cameron said. "We stay on their trail."

Before Tori could reply, another shot was heard. Tori flinched and Cameron grabbed her arm again.

"We're still a couple of hours behind them, Hunter. You think we're the only people out on this mountain? That could be anybody. We've got to stay focused."

Andrea wished she could take solace in Cameron's words. But she didn't. And she knew Tori Hunter didn't either. They were in the middle of nowhere, not close to a trail. The chances of that gunshot being from a third party was slight. She knew it. Cameron knew it. And most likely Tori knew it.

"Come on."

Tori nodded but didn't speak. Andrea noted her clenched jaw, the hands that were balled into fists. She could only imagine what she was thinking.

* * *

Sam shook her head. "I'm not sure that I can do it."

"They taste like chicken, Sam."

Sam looked at the two squirrels he held up by the tails. Cute, fuzzy little squirrels. She looked back at Angel skeptically.

"You ate the fish," he reminded her.

"Yeah, fish. Not cute little squirrels."

"Think of them as rodents then."

She laughed. "Oh, yeah. That's helping my appetite right there, Angel."

"Well, there's some more of that beef stew you like so much," he said as he pulled out his knife. "I'm going to clean and skin them. You don't have to eat them if you don't want."

"We'll see."

She went about gathering wood for their fire. There was still a little daylight left and she was surprised that he'd stopped already. Not that she was complaining. The last hour had them steadily climbing and her legs were like jelly.

She looked back from where they'd come. It was an endless sea of trees and brush, smatterings of rocks and open spaces. The stream they were camped at was little more than a spring. The water was cool and clear, but barely three feet wide. No chance for fish. But it would allow her to clean up even if it wasn't wide or deep enough for a bath. Her gaze left the stream and slid to where Angel had gone downstream to clean the squirrels. She wasn't sure what was the least appetizing—the horrid beef stew or the idea of eating a squirrel.

CHAPTER FIFTEEN

Tori absently poked the fire with a stick, watching as the embers rose then disappeared. It was a still night and the smoke twirled directly overhead. She was aware of Andrea watching her, but she kept her eyes on the fire. Her dinner—a freeze-dried beef stroganoff that didn't look half bad—was sitting beside her, largely untouched. The knot in her stomach wouldn't allow her to eat.

As Cameron had said, the gunshots they'd heard could have been from anyone. But in her gut, she knew that wasn't true. And by Cameron's and Andrea's demeanor, they knew it too. As much as she wanted to stay positive, as much as she wanted to believe that Sam was okay, she had to face the fact that Sam was a hostage, held by a killer. A man who had gone on a killing spree and in one day had murdered at least eleven people, including his own team. That told her he had no loyalty to anyone. And that also told her that Sam was in grave danger. The shots they'd heard today reminded her of that.

She refused to believe that he'd killed Sam. No. She couldn't even *think* that. Maybe the shots had been a warning. Maybe Sam had tried to escape.

Andrea stirred and Tori glanced over at her. As expected, Andrea's eyes were on her. In the firelight, Tori recognized the sympathetic look in them. Andrea surely knew what thoughts were flying around in her mind. But Tori said nothing and neither did Andrea. Cameron too had been quiet. And really, what could they say?

Nothing.

So she sat there alone, silently brooding over the possibility that something might have happened to Sam. If Sam was taken from her, she thought her very soul might likely die right then and there. Would she revert back to the old ways? Would she shut herself off from everyone? Would she go back into the darkness that had swallowed her up after her family's murder?

She would try, surely. But she knew Casey and Leslie wouldn't let her. They loved her. They would keep her sane. She would try to hide from them too, but she knew O'Connor would badger her until she let them back in.

She shook her head, hating the direction of her thoughts. Sam was okay. She had to be. She just had to be.

* * *

"Okay, so it does taste a little like chicken," Sam said as she pulled the meat from the bone. "A little."

"Beats that beef stew, doesn't it?" Angel asked as he put another small limb on their fire.

"For sure." She stopped chewing for a moment, watching him as he sipped from his water bottle. He was staring at her, and she raised her eyebrows questioningly.

"Where did you grow up?"

The question was unexpected. While she'd peppered him with questions during their daily hikes, he rarely asked her anything. Usually only about Tori and their relationship.

"My family is from Denver," she said. She sighed. "We're not really that close. My brother…well, he's all that matters to them. I was pretty much invisible."

"Why is that?"

"He's a priest. No matter what I did, I could never measure up to that."

"A priest, huh?" He smiled. "How did they take you being gay?"

Sam shook her head. "That was pretty much the last straw. Being a cop didn't go over too well to begin with. But when I brought Tori home to meet them…well, let's just say there was a lot of praying involved," she said with a laugh.

"So you don't see them?"

"No. We talk on the phone a couple of times a year, that's about it." She shrugged. "My brother…we don't really have a relationship at all." He handed her another part of the squirrel and she took it. "What about you? Where did you grow up?"

He surprised her by answering as easily as he did. "Around here, actually."

"New Mexico? Or *here*?"

"Taos."

"Wow. So you've been on these mountains before?"

"I was a kid. We moved to California when I was twelve," he said. "Everything I know about this mountain is from research only."

"Like where the streams are?"

"Yes."

"Why did you move to California?"

He poked the fire with a stick, a thoughtful expression on his face. "My father lost his job here. Again." He laid the stick on top of the flames. "I told you he drank. He had a hard time keeping jobs. He had an uncle in California. Offered him a job. So we moved." Angel shrugged. "Not much changed though."

From what he'd said, this would have been four years before his mother was killed. She was curious about his childhood but decided to keep things more current.

"Are you ever going to tell me what you did?"

"What I did?"

"Yeah, what you did," she said. "You must have done something. When you killed that family, you said you needed a distraction. Why? And why would you need a hostage?"

He looked away from her, and for the first time, she thought she saw remorse—even shame—in his expression. Like other questions she'd asked him, she didn't expect to get an answer right away. She normally had to prompt him to get him to talk.

"It was a really long day," he said, his voice quiet in the muted darkness. "I had everything planned out. Even a couple of contingency plans too." He looked back at her. "Because something could always go wrong. The more people you have involved, the more chance of a mishap. So I am operating on one of those contingency plans now."

She waited, hoping he would continue without her having to ask.

"The military trained me for one thing. That was to kill. And I was very good at my job. I also learned that I could make a lot of money doing it for the private sector instead of the military."

"Like a hit man?"

"Yeah. I worked the Middle East, mostly. Europe. Sometimes Asia. But I'm ready to retire from this line of work. This job gave me the opportunity to do that."

She was almost afraid to ask. But she did anyway. "What job?"

"My contract was to…eliminate a guy. He happened to work for an armored car company."

"What did he do? Why did someone want him killed?"

Angel shook his head. "I don't ask, they don't tell. I don't need to know the why of it."

"So what happened?"

"My plan was to make the hit while he was at work. And then to relieve his company of several million dollars. Which meant I needed a team."

"You work alone?"

"Always. In my line of work, you can't afford mistakes."

Sam nodded. "So I take it, there were mistakes then?"

"My first mistake was hiring two ex-military guys who thought they were smarter than me," he said. "I had the company staked out. I knew the routine. I'd stashed a car about a mile from the place. I had a man there waiting for us. The guard I had the hit on, his shift started at five in the morning. I knew his routine as well. He always showed up a few minutes after the first guard. We needed both of their codes to access the building." He glanced over at her. "Without going into all the details, we got away with the armored car full of cash. I'm guessing about three million. We unloaded the cash into our car and headed to Taos. That's where things broke down."

"The two guys who thought they were smarter than you?"

"Yeah. They thought they would just take all the money for themselves."

"So you killed them?"

"Yes. And left the car."

"And the money?"

He laughed. "Hell, no. There were five of us. Three now. We stole a car, took the money and headed out again. But we were behind schedule and there was nothing discreet about our getaway. There were cops everywhere."

"So you needed a distraction," Sam said.

He stared at her. "Yes, I needed a distraction. I needed several distractions. And I needed to hide the money and get rid of my remaining team."

"Oh."

"I told you, Sam, I'm a killer."

"Yes, you did. I haven't forgotten."

CHAPTER SIXTEEN

Cameron thought they were gaining ground, but she didn't know for sure, not until she felt the ashes of their most recent campfire.

"Still warm," she said. "I'm guessing not much more than an hour, less than two."

"So we might catch them today?" Tori asked.

"If we don't have any setbacks, we might," she said. She pointed to the small stream. "Fill up if you need to."

"Hey, guys," Andrea said. "I think I found the reason for the gunshots we heard."

Cameron and Tori walked over to her, watching as she kicked at a small pile of bones.

"What is it?" Tori asked.

"Squirrel, most likely," Cameron said.

Andrea nodded. "Looks like they had fresh meat for dinner."

Tori shook her head. "No way would Sam eat that."

"Two squirrels. We heard two shots."

"If you're hungry, you'll eat just about anything," Cameron said. "I speak from experience." She heard the low rumble of a helicopter and looked at her watch. "Right on time."

"How close will they get?" Tori asked.

"Not much closer. Just enough to make him think they're searching for him."

"You really think he's heading toward the highway?"

Cameron knelt down near the stream and filled her water bottle. "Eventually. He's been traveling parallel with it. He could turn north at any time and hit the highway within half a day, I'd think."

Tori splashed water on her face, then on her hair and slicked it back. "I can't wait to get a shower," she said.

"You and me both," Andrea said. She looked at Cameron. "How did you stand going weeks without a bath?"

"Weeks?" Tori asked. "Really?"

Cameron nodded. "I spent three months in the desert with little provisions. Water was for drinking only." She stood up. "Ready to head out?"

"Yeah. Let's catch this bastard," Tori said.

* * *

"Helicopters again," Sam said. "They still don't sound very close though."

Angel's gaze went to the sky. "No. They must be checking grid by grid."

"I must not hold much weight as a hostage," she said. "I'd like to think there'd be a hundred helicopters out looking for me."

He gave a quick laugh. "Sorry to bust your bubble, kid, but right now, I'd guess they're more interested in me than you."

"Because you have three million dollars?"

"Well, that, and they have a morgue full of bodies."

Oh, yeah. Sam had to remind herself sometimes what he'd done. Since that first day, he'd treated her more like a hiking companion than a hostage. And she, in turn, had started to think of him as something other than a killer and kidnapper. That was a bit disturbing.

"What will you do if they get closer? The helicopters, I mean."

"We'll take cover."

"Yeah, but what if they have heat-seeking imaging technology?"

He shook his head. "You've watched too many movies, Sam."

"Come on, Angel. You were military. Even in Dallas, we have the capability."

"Sounds like they're using a search and rescue helicopter. It's not military though, which is surprising."

"How do you know it's not?"

"I just do."

Sam trudged after him. He seemed to be in a bit more of a hurry today. And while her sense of direction wasn't great, she felt like they'd turned. Of course, which way, she couldn't tell. She looked up, finding the sun. Maybe they were heading to the north or northwest now. She opened her mouth to ask, then closed it. He didn't seem to be in a talkative mood today. Maybe the helicopters had him more spooked than he let on. He appeared to be all business now. That frightened her a little.

Okay…a lot.

CHAPTER SEVENTEEN

Tori knew their day would be coming to an end soon. Clouds had built up to the west, obscuring the sun. Even if there were no clouds, she knew the sun was dangerously close to slipping behind the mountain anyway. Once it did, she knew Cameron would slow their pace to make sure she didn't lose the trail. With the thick clouds overhead, it was only a matter of time before she called a halt to their travel.

And there was still no sign of Sam.

Each time they crested a ridge, each time they came to a vast clearing, Cameron got her binoculars out and scanned the area. Nothing. Cameron thought they were getting close and Tori felt it too. She could almost sense Sam's presence nearby.

Her apprehension had faded only a little after finding the bones of what Cameron had said were squirrels. It could have explained the shots they heard. And Cameron said Sam was still leaving evidence along their trail, pointing out an overturned rock or a broken limb, however subtle it may be. So surely Sam was okay.

But how much time did she have? If Angel was heading to the highway, would he try to steal a car? Would he take Sam with him? Or would he feel safe and no longer need her?

For that matter, did he ever really need her at all? They hadn't been close to catching him. Why was he still hanging on to Sam? What purpose had she served him?

She had no answers to her questions, and she followed behind Andrea silently. All too soon, she noticed their pace had slowed. Cameron was being careful not to lose the trail.

"We'll have to stop soon," Cameron said unnecessarily.

Tori didn't comment.

* * *

Sam sat silently by the fire, eating a pasta dish that wasn't too bad. It wasn't as horrible as the beef stew but it did remind her how good the fish...and even the squirrel had been. Angel had been unusually quiet, even for him. Her attempt at conversation was usually met with curt answers or no comment at all. She had finally taken the hint and stopped talking. She was surprised he'd stopped to make camp as early as he had.

There was no stream here, but they'd passed one a few hours earlier where they'd filled their water bottles. It was a flat, grassy area surrounded by rather large pines. They'd left the junipers behind again. He already had their tent up, a safe distance away from the fire.

"Looks like rain tonight," he said, breaking the silence.

His voice startled her as it was the first words he'd spoken since they'd made camp. When he'd stopped, he'd gone about the business of setting up the tent. She'd collected firewood, as had become the norm. She'd tried not to let his silence frighten her, but his mood had definitely changed.

"It feels cooler than normal," she said, contributing to the conversation.

"You can use the sleeping bag tonight," he offered.

She smiled at him. "And what will you use?"

"I'll use your coat, like you've been."

She tilted her head. "Why have you been so quiet?"

He met her eyes across the fire but said nothing.

Oh.

She looked away from him, her appetite disappearing. She attempted another couple of bites before putting the container down. She closed her eyes for a moment, wondering where Tori was.

And wondering how much time she had left. The look in his eyes frightened her a little. And frightened was something she had not truly been in several days.

CHAPTER EIGHTEEN

Sam was cold and she pulled the sleeping bag up higher around her neck. Angel had already gotten up, saying he would get a fire going. The rain that had threatened had finally hit during the night, a brief downpour with thunder off in the distance. Light rain ensued, the quiet tap, tap, tap on the tent lulling her to sleep.

The rain had ended earlier, and she saw streaks of sunlight slashing across the tent now. She sat up suddenly. By the time the sun was this high, they would have already been on the trail.

"Fire's hot," he called.

Something wasn't right. This wasn't their routine. The apprehension she'd been trying to push aside hit her full force this morning. She unzipped the tent, finding him kneeling by the fire, his hands held out to its warmth.

He glanced at her, and she thought she actually saw a smile in his eyes. He appeared relaxed this morning, showing none of the tension that he had yesterday. He motioned around them.

"What do you think? Nice, huh?"

She looked around, not understanding his question. Then she took a deep breath and it hit her. The forest was alive with smells she hadn't experienced before. She held her arms out to the side, breathing deeply again.

"Oh, my God, that's wonderful. It smells like vanilla or...or maybe butterscotch," she said as she turned in a circle. "What is it?"

He pointed at one of the huge pines near the tent. "Stick your nose against the bark of that ponderosa there."

Sam went to it, feeling like a tree hugger as she wrapped her arms around it and took a deep breath. She actually moaned at the intoxicating smell. She released the tree and looked around. Everything was damp and fresh and clean from the rain. The sun was streaking through the trees, warming the air around her already.

"It's a glorious morning," she said with a smile. "Beautiful."

"Yeah. I'm glad you think so." He stood up, staring at her, the smile leaving his face. "Because...it's time, Sam. It's time we part company."

She stared at him, feeling her heart tighten in her chest. "Oh. I see." She turned her back to him quickly, her eyes darting around frantically. "Is this where I should make a run for it so that you can shoot me in the back?" She turned around to face him again, meeting his gaze. "Or do you want to do it while I'm looking at you?" She felt tears in her eyes, and she tried to blink them away. "Either way, I'd prefer the gun to your knife. I have this...this thing with knives," she said with a quick shake of her head.

He walked toward her and reached out a hand, and she flinched from his touch.

"God, Sam...I'm not going to shoot you."

"Please, Angel, not the knife," she whispered.

He held his hands up. "Sam, I'm not going to hurt you."

She stared at him, confused. "But you said—"

"I know what I said. But you've...well, you've..." he said, not finishing his thought. "Maybe my old, hard heart is softening up. I'm not going to kill you, but I can't take you with me. You'll be safer here than with me."

"The road?"

He nodded. "Yes. It's about a two-, three-hour hike, at the most."

She should have been flooded with relief. But…"You're going to leave me here? Alone?"

"Yes. If someone is coming for you like you think, then you'll be fine."

"But—"

"You'll be fine, Sam. I'll leave the tent. I'll leave food and water. You'll be fine," he said again. "And if someone doesn't come in the next day or so, then you head for the highway." He took her shoulders and turned her around. "See that peak?" he asked, pointing ahead of them. "That's Wheeler Peak. Keep it to your right, like it is now. Just head north. You'll hit the highway."

"What highway? I don't even know where we are."

"It's the highway to Taos. This many days, they won't still have roadblocks up anymore." He walked back to the fire. "Come on. Let's have some breakfast, then I need to get going."

She nodded and noticed that he already had water boiling. She sat next to him near the fire and sipped a cup of instant coffee as he got the powdered eggs started. She had so many thoughts running through her mind, she couldn't settle on any one of them. He was leaving her. He wasn't going to kill her.

He held his hand out to her. "Here. For your fire tonight."

She took the matches from him and nodded. "Thank you."

They ate in silence, although their glances collided often. She had no idea what to say in a situation like this. Before long, he stood up and she knew it was time. She got up too, starting to clean up their breakfast.

"Remember not to take food or trash into the tent with you," he said.

She nodded. "You don't think a…a mountain lion will come, do you?"

"I'm sorry I said that. No, you'll be fine."

She wished she believed him.

He surprised her by pulling her into a quick hug. So quick that she had no time to react before he released her.

"I'm sorry for what I put you through, Sam. I truly am. If I had to do it over again," he said. "Well…taking a hostage wasn't one of my better ideas."

She met his gaze head-on. "I guess I should say thank you for not killing me and wish you good luck…but I am a cop," she said and shrugged apologetically.

He smiled. "I know. I'll simply pretend that you said it. How's that?"

She smiled too. "I do mean the 'thank you' part sincerely though."

He pointed to a couple of rations of food he'd tossed on the ground. "You'll be okay, Sam. Don't worry too much," he said as he slipped on his backpack.

Her gaze landed on the rations. "Beef stew? Really, Angel?"

"Sorry. It's all we've got left." Then he handed her an energy bar. "For lunch. And go easy on the water, it's all you've got."

She stared at him. "You're worried about me," she stated.

"Yeah. Don't tell anyone. It'll totally ruin my reputation."

And with that, he gave her a quick nod and nearly sprinted into the forest, leaving her behind to watch as he disappeared into the trees.

She blew out her breath, then looked around her. Birds flitted in the trees nearby and she listened to their calls. The fragrant smell of the forest invaded her senses and she felt peacefulness settle around her.

She was totally alone.

And she was alive and safe.

A quick smile turned into a laugh. But that faded quickly. She turned, looking back to where they'd come from yesterday.

"Come on, Tori. Where are you?" she murmured.

CHAPTER NINETEEN

Tori stared into the damp forest as Cameron tried to get a head on their trail. The rain had "wreaked havoc on the goddamn marks," Cameron had stated as she walked back and forth, trying to find something.

Oh, Sam…where are you?

Tori turned, watching Cameron, practically willing her to find something—anything—to indicate the route Sam had taken. Andrea touched her arm and Tori turned toward her.

"She'll find it."

She nodded. Time was wasting, Tori knew, but it wasn't Cameron's fault it had rained last night. She wondered how Sam had slept? Was he keeping her in a tent with him? Or did he tie her to a tree at night? Was she out in the cold and rain? She clenched her fists, vowing—for the hundredth time—that she would shoot the bastard the first time she laid eyes on him. That is, if Cameron didn't beat her to it.

"Okay, I think I got it," Cameron said. She was at least thirty feet ahead of them, on a rocky incline. "Finally found some overturned rocks here."

Tori headed her way, glancing where Cameron had pointed. How Cameron could be sure that was the trail, she had no idea. But she followed and only six feet later, Cameron pointed out another rut in the dirt.

"Because of the rain, a lot was washed away on this slope," she explained. "Hopefully, if the trail levels out, it'll be easier to follow." She looked back at Tori. "I know we're going slow. I'm sorry."

Tori was surprised by the apology. "I'd rather go slow and be sure," she said, knowing that was a contradiction to how she'd felt when they first started out on this manhunt. Then, she'd wanted to dash about haphazardly and start calling for Sam. It's something she wanted to do right now, in fact.

"I emailed Murdock our coordinates," Cameron said. "According to my GPS, we're not far from the highway." She turned back around and glanced at her. "If we don't catch up to them in a couple of hours, then…"

"Then you think he'll have gotten to the highway? Taken Sam?"

"I'm just saying, if they reach the highway and get a car, then our part of this chase is over. Murdock will have patrols along this stretch of highway. If he hits the road, they'll find him."

And then Sam could be involved in a shootout. She could already picture some overanxious deputy, not used to this much action, pulling his weapon and trying to take out Angel, regardless of the consequences. Sam could end up shot. She could end up dead.

"Then let's catch up to them first," Andrea said, pushing Tori along the trail.

Tori nodded a silent thank-you to Andrea, shoving her morbid thoughts aside. Sam would be fine.

She had to be.

* * *

Sam paced back and forth between the tent and the campfire. She'd let the fire die down as the sun had chased the morning chill away. Of course, she had no idea what time it was. In fact, she didn't even know what day it was anymore. Sunday? Monday?

She thought of the others—Casey and Leslie. If Leslie was okay, had they headed back to Dallas? Knowing Tori, she would have sent them away. But who was out looking for her? The sheriff's department? And where the hell were the helicopters they'd heard? Surely to God *someone* was out looking for her.

Yes, of course they were.

But right now, being alone like this, she felt doubt creep in. Was it as Angel had thought? They were looking for them on the highway and not out here on the mountain?

She blew out her breath and leaned against a pine, sliding down its length until she was sitting on the ground. How long had Angel been gone? An hour? Two? She stared off into the clearing, trying to reconcile her feelings for him. He was a killer. Yes. She saw firsthand what he'd done. He'd *told* her what all he'd done.

But…he had become…what? Her protector? She shook her head. No, he was her abductor. She had been at his mercy. And for some reason, he hadn't kept his promise to kill her when he no longer needed her.

She knew why, of course. She had become a person to him, not a target. She was real. She had become a part of his life, if only for a few days. In turn, he had become a part of hers. And in the end, he couldn't bring himself to kill her. She wasn't sure when things had changed. Was it when they'd gone fishing? Maybe before that, even. But regardless, he was still a killer.

And he was still on the run.

She picked up a twig that was lying beside her and she snapped it in two, then snapped it again, breaking it up absently as she continued to stare out past the trees, seeing nothing, hearing nothing.

* * *

Tori waited as patiently as she could as Cameron walked back and forth across the pine needles. Tori knew Cameron was frustrated. Hell, they were all frustrated. Their pace had slowed to a crawl as Cameron kept losing the trail.

"I got nothing," Cameron said. "No footprints, no overturned rocks, no broken limbs, nothing. Goddamn rain," she said for the fifth time.

"What about this?" Andrea asked. "Broken tip here," she said, fingering a low-growing bush.

Tori and Cameron both walked over to where she was and Cameron touched it too, studying it. She stepped back, looking at the ground around the bush. Nothing looked disturbed.

"I lost the trail back there, about thirty feet," she said. "A bed of pine needles. He could have used that as a cover to change directions."

"And Sam broke the limb to let us know," Tori said, nodding.

Cameron pulled out her GPS gadget again and turned around, apparently trying to find their bearings. She walked to her right, ten feet, then twenty before stopping.

"Here," she said.

There was an old, rotted limb that had been kicked over, exposing the moist earth beneath it.

"This makes sense," Cameron said. "He's turned finally. Heading directly for the highway."

"Then let's go already," Tori said, feeling a tug of urgency. They were close. Real close. She could feel it.

Cameron led them on again, her pace still too slow for Tori's liking. She felt like she was pushing Cameron along as she was right at her heels. She could feel Andrea close behind her.

"You on my back won't get us there any faster," Cameron said without turning around.

"Sorry. But Sam's close by. I feel it."

"While I appreciate your sixth sense, I'm still staying on their trail like we've been doing."

Tori kept her mouth shut but didn't slow her pace. She felt her anxiety build, felt her pulse start to race. Yes, Sam was close by.

A mere ten minutes later, they broke into a clearing and they all stopped up short as a bright yellow tent came into view. Cameron quickly ducked back into the trees, pulling Tori with her.

"Could be a trap," she said as she pulled out her binoculars.

Tori stared through the branches of the pine they were hiding behind, her breath catching as she spied Sam sitting against a tree.

"Sam," she murmured. She felt relief flood her. "She's there."

She was about to bolt in that direction when Cameron's strong arm held her in place.

"Goddamn it, Hunter. Will you wait? Angel is around here somewhere."

"No. Sam would warn us."

Tori kept her gaze fixed on Sam and saw Sam tilt her head as if listening.

"She's knows I'm here," Tori said quietly.

"We're hidden," Cameron said as she searched the area with her binoculars. "She hasn't seen us."

"I'm telling you, she knows I'm here."

Sam turned then, looking directly at them.

"Well, I'll be goddamned," Cameron murmured.

"We have this…this thing," Tori said.

"Stay hidden," Cameron said. "Andrea, watch our back. Angel could have circled around."

"Yes, I got it."

But Sam stood, her gaze still seemingly locked on them. Tori felt her heart beating rapidly in her chest.

"Tori?" Sam called loudly, her voice echoing in the trees. She took a step in their direction. "Tori?"

"Fuck this," Tori muttered as she stepped out from behind the tree. "Sam!"

Sam took off running in her direction and Tori let her pack slip from her shoulders as she bolted toward Sam, ignoring Cameron's call for her to wait. Their eyes met as Sam ran toward her and even though Tori tried to brace herself, when Sam flung herself into her arms she very nearly toppled them.

"Oh, Sam," Tori said, wrapping her tightly in her arms. "My God, Sam."

"You came," Sam said as she buried her face against Tori's neck. "I knew you would."

Tori felt Sam cling to her as if a lifeline and she held her tightly.

"Are you okay?" she asked urgently.

"Yes. Hold me for a second, okay. Please, just hold me."

"I got you," Tori said, squeezing Sam almost painfully tight.

"I was so scared," Sam said.

"Me too. God, me too." She squeezed her eyes shut. "Did he…did he hurt you?"

Sam pulled back slightly, meeting her worried stare. She shook her head. "No." She leaned closer and they kissed, quick and hard, nearly desperate, then Sam tucked her head against her breasts.

"Thank God," Tori said. "I was so worried about you. God, Sam, I love you. I was so worried."

"I love you too. So much."

Tori squeezed her tight again, finally admitting to herself that she'd been terrified that she'd never get to hold Sam again.

"How's Leslie?" Sam murmured against her chest.

"She's okay," Tori said.

Tori heard Cameron and Andrea approach, and she pulled out of Sam's embrace, although she didn't let go of her. Sam turned to them.

"Who are you?"

Tori motioned to them. "FBI. This is Special Agent—"

But Andrea interrupted her formal introduction. "I'm Andrea Sullivan. This is Cameron Ross."

Sam shook both of their hands. "Thank you for finding me."

"It was Cameron's doing," Tori admitted. "She was tracking you."

"You left a lot of clues," Cameron said. She looked toward the tent. "Where is he?"

"Angel? He left this morning."

"Left?"

"He was heading to the highway, he said. I'm assuming toward Taos." She turned and pointed into the forest. "He went that way."

Cameron's gaze followed her direction, then she looked back at Sam. "No offense, but it's not like Angel to leave loose ends."

Sam shrugged. "Well, we kinda…bonded."

"Bonded? What do you mean?" Tori asked sharply.

Sam looked at her. "I don't know. I mean, we talked. We… talked. At the end, I think he couldn't bring himself to…to kill me." Sam met her eyes. "Which is what he promised he'd do when he first took me."

Cameron pulled out her GPS gadget and turned a semicircle, finally stopping as she faced away from them. "Looks like we're about two hours from the highway."

"Yes, that's what he thought too," Sam said.

Cameron pocketed the GPS quickly and pointed toward the tent. "Break camp. We're going after him. We won't catch him before he gets to the highway, but at least we'll know where he hit it. I'll call Murdock and get someone to pick us up there." She pulled out her phone and was already walking away when she looked back at them. "You need to be debriefed," she said, pointing at Sam.

Sam nodded. "I know."

Tori stepped forward. "No, Cameron. She's been through enough. She needs some downtime. *We* need some downtime."

"I don't care what you need, Hunter. He's killed eleven that we know of. If we're going to catch him, we need to pick her brain."

Cameron walked off with the phone held to her ear.

Tori turned to Sam, reaching out and touching her face. "I don't really like her very much. She's arrogant and bossy as hell."

Sam smiled and patted Tori's chest. "I bet you two got along famously then," she teased.

Tori heard Andrea's quiet laugh behind them and turned, smiling at her. "Yeah. Andrea can attest to that."

Andrea pointed at the tent. "I'll take it down."

When she walked away, Tori pulled Sam into another hug. "You sure you're okay?"

"Yes, I'm fine."

They went to help Andrea, then Tori bumped her shoulder playfully. "Did you really eat a squirrel?"

CHAPTER TWENTY

Andrea actually moaned as she stood under the warm spray of water in their shower. It was glorious. She heard Cameron on the phone and assumed it was Murdock getting an update.

They'd been picked up at the highway and taken back to the campground where their motorhome was parked. Tori and Sam were being put up in one of the cabins that the Forest Service rented out. Cameron had given them two hours of downtime. Then they were to all four meet for Sam's debriefing.

The only sign of Angel Figueroa had been tire tracks leaving the forest and heading onto the highway. He'd apparently had a car stashed there. Why he'd killed that family and abducted Sam to trek across the mountain to a car was anyone's guess. Cameron hoped Sam could shed some light on Angel's plan based on any conversations they may have had.

But right now, she didn't want to think about it. Right now, she wanted to relish her shower. She had just rinsed the shampoo from her hair when she heard the bathroom door open. She smiled as she pictured Cameron contemplating joining her.

They'd tried that before but the motorhome's shower was a bit too small for both of them.

"Saving me some hot water?"

"Only if I have to," she said as she turned the water off. Cameron was holding her towel and Andrea stepped from the shower, meeting Cameron's eyes as she took it. "Your turn."

"You know, if I hurry, we'll have some time before they get here."

Andrea grinned as she moved to the side. "Then by all means hurry."

* * *

Sam's eyes closed as Tori's lips nibbled below her ear, and she let a quiet moan slip out. They didn't really have time for this, but they needed this closeness, they needed to reconnect.

"I love you," Tori whispered against her skin. "And I was so afraid I wouldn't ever get to tell you that again."

Sam's eyes fluttered open for a second, then closed again. She smiled, her hands moving across Tori's bare back to hold her closer.

"I knew you would find me," she murmured. "I never doubted it. It was like...I could feel you coming for me."

Tori raised her head. "If Cameron hadn't been there, I don't know if I could have found you. She was good." Tori's hand moved lazily between her breasts. "I was...I was terrified of what he was doing to you."

Sam touched her cheek, letting her thumb rake across her lips. "He didn't hurt me, sweetheart. The first night...well, I was afraid he would. But he didn't touch me."

Tori met her eyes. "When you said you'd bonded with him...what does that mean?"

Sam sighed. She had been wondering when Tori would bring that up. "I'm not sure," she said truthfully. "At first, he was all business. He told me he would kill me when he didn't need me anymore. I believed him. But we started talking. Both of us. And at the end, I was Sam, a person. Not merely some random woman he'd abducted. I think he thought of me almost as a friend."

"He left you his tent."

"And food and water," she said. "Tori, I know what he did. I know he's a killer. I haven't lost sight of that. But with me, he was almost a gentleman. And I admit, when he left, I had a hard time reconciling the Angel that I knew with the man who had killed so many."

Tori nodded. "Cameron will want to know everything you talked about."

"I know." She closed her eyes again and pulled Tori into a kiss. "But I don't want to talk about it right now," she said. "I want you to make love to me. I want to forget about it for a little while. Take me away for a few minutes."

Tori ducked her head, her tongue lightly touching one nipple. Sam took a deep breath, trying to chase thoughts of Angel from her mind. Tori's familiar touch did just that.

CHAPTER TWENTY-ONE

Cameron stole a pepperoni from the pizza as Andrea took it out of the box. The nearest café had loaded them up with burgers and fries to go, but Andrea had surprised her by getting a pizza too.

"Figured you were having withdrawals," Andrea said.

"Yes. I could eat the whole thing myself," she said. She looked at her watch. "They should have been here by now."

"They're at the mercy of the ranger, remember. It's not like they have a car," Andrea reminded her.

Cameron scooped up Lola as she was about to jump on the counter to inspect the pizza. "No, you don't," she said. "That's mine."

Andrea moved the plates aside, then bent down and kissed Lola on the head. "I missed her."

"Yeah, me too."

Andrea took Lola from her and let her slip to the ground, then moved closer, looping her arms across Cameron's shoulders. "And I missed *us*," Andrea said as she kissed her.

Cameron smiled against her lips. "I know. We haven't had much alone time." She kissed her again. "Earlier was kinda nice."

"Uh-huh."

"Since Angel is on the run, Murdock may bring in another team. We might be able to get out of here. Head back north to the mountains."

Andrea pulled back. "Really? I thought he'd want us to finish it."

"Our mission was to rescue Samantha Kennedy, not apprehend Angel," she said. "Of course, we didn't so much as rescue her as Angel left her behind." She stepped away from Andrea with a shake of her head. "And like I told her, it's not like him to leave loose ends. She's damn lucky."

"But?"

"But something doesn't feel right," she said. "Why did he take her in the first place? He could have disappeared into the mountains on his own."

"Maybe he didn't know that," Andrea said. "Maybe he thought someone was right behind him, tracking him from the beginning."

"Knowing Angel, he was probably just taking precautions. And if he did have a car stashed out there, then this was Plan B, or even C," she said. "He's not in the military anymore, but I'm sure he's remembered his training. Every mission, you always have a backup plan that's as detailed and as practiced as the original."

"What about—" But a knock on the door interrupted her and she frowned. "No alarm?"

Cameron smiled as she went to open it. "I didn't want to scare them. Or make them think that I'm paranoid," she added with a quick laugh.

Tori and Sam stood outside, and Cameron motioned for them to enter.

"The ranger," Tori said. "He wanted to know if he needed to pick us up later."

"No, we'll take you back to your cabin," Cameron said. "Come on in."

Tori waved the ranger off, then followed Sam inside. Sam was already looking around.

"Wow. This is so much bigger than the one we rented," Sam said. "Nice."

"Only this is not rented," Tori said. "FBI owns it."

"Really?" Sam looked at Cameron questioningly. "Sorry. I don't know the history."

"This is our home," Andrea said. "And office."

"Our assignments are mostly remote," Cameron explained.

"Beats the hell out of an office in the city," Sam said with a smile.

"Yes." She turned to Tori. "So…everything okay? Downtime helped?" She was surprised by the subtle blush on Tori's face.

"Yes, it was very nice."

"Great." She glanced at Andrea and smiled. "Our downtime was too."

Sam laughed and linked arms with Tori. "I like this FBI team much more than the one you have in Dallas."

"Figured you would," Tori said with a quick glance at Cameron.

"I hope you're hungry," Andrea said. "We picked up burgers and a loaded pizza."

"Oh, God, yes," Sam said. "We're starving. Let me help."

Cameron looked at Tori. "You want to see my computers?"

"The ones you don't know how to use?"

Cameron scowled. "I know how to use most of them."

"I know you want to show off your toys," Andrea said with a smile, "but can we eat first?"

"Of course," she said. "That pizza's been calling my name."

"I know it has," Andrea said as she opened the bag of burgers. "Sam, if you could get the fries out of the oven. I put them in there to keep warm."

"What can I do?" Tori asked.

"Grab us a beer," Cameron said as she bit into a piece of pizza before putting a burger on her plate.

The motorhome was a little crowded with all four of them, but they soon settled down to eat. Cameron sat in her recliner and Tori took the love seat. Andrea and Sam sat at the small dinette.

"Excellent burger," Sam said. "I didn't realize how much I missed real food."

"I still can't believe you ate a squirrel," Tori said.

"Angel caught a trout too. That beat the hell out of the beef stew he served."

"MREs?" Cameron asked.

"Yes. The powdered eggs for breakfast kinda grew on me though."

Cameron decided now was as good a time as any to question Sam. She thought it would be less of an interrogation this way. She decided to start at the beginning.

"Did Angel say anything to you when he first...well, when he abducted you?"

Sam nodded. "Yes. When I asked him what he wanted, he said a hostage. He said in exchange, he wouldn't cut Leslie's throat," she said with a quick glance at Tori.

"Did he say why he needed a hostage?"

"He said it was to prevent you from coming after him with guns blazing. I think those are the words he used," Sam said. "I told him it would be a lot quicker for him to disappear without me slowing him down, but he didn't go for that," she added with a smile.

Cameron was surprised by her composure. She wasn't certain what she'd been expecting, but Sam didn't appear to be any worse for wear after her ordeal.

"Did you try to escape?" Andrea asked.

Sam shook her head. "No. Well, I mean I thought about it several times. But what would I do? He could outrun me. He had a gun. He had a knife. My hands were bound at the wrists for the first two days. I was tied to him with a rope." She paused. "Well, at first. I guess after the mountain lion scare he thought it was a pretty safe bet I wouldn't make a run for it."

"What mountain lion?" Tori asked. "You didn't say—"

"No, I mean he said if I ran off a mountain lion would have me for dinner." Sam smiled again. "Every noise I heard, I imagined it was a mountain lion stalking us." She looked directly at Cameron. "I must sound pretty pathetic for a cop. I mean, I didn't even try to disarm him."

Cameron shook her head. "Angel Figueroa is an expert in martial arts. He knows every trick in the book on how to kill someone. You could not have disarmed him, Sam."

Sam's gaze never wavered from hers. "How do you know him?"

"We served in the military together. We were on the same team for a while."

Sam nodded. "You were a sniper too?"

Cameron was surprised she knew that. Apparently the look on her face said as much.

"We talked," Sam said. "He told me what he did in the military."

Sam took another bite of her burger, and Cameron wondered if it was to allow her time to collect her thoughts. After a moment, Sam took a swallow of beer, then let out a rather heavy sigh.

"At first, he wouldn't tell me his name. He just kept reiterating that when he had no more use for me, he would kill me." Sam looked quickly at Tori. "And I believed him. And I knew that I needed to become more than only a nameless hostage to him. So I talked. I told him my name, I told him about Tori. I told him that I was a cop." She shrugged. "He finally told me his name. I asked him a ton of questions, most of which he ignored. At first." Sam looked at Cameron again. "When we didn't hear helicopters searching, he assumed you thought we were on the highway and that you had roadblocks set up. When we finally heard the helicopters, he thought it was because the roadblocks hadn't panned out."

Cameron glanced over at Tori with raised eyebrows, and Tori laughed.

"Okay, fine. You were right."

Cameron grinned. "Of course I was. You should never doubt me."

"Right about what?" Sam asked.

"They had a little argument over whether or not they should send helicopters out right away," Andrea explained. "Cameron wanted to wait, hoping it would confuse Angel."

"And Tori wanted to send out the National Guard to look for me, no doubt," Sam said with smile.

"That I did," Tori agreed.

Cameron got up and grabbed another slice of pizza. "So did he tell you what he'd done? I mean, did you know why he was running?"

"He eventually told me, yes. I mean, I knew he'd killed that girl. He told me he'd killed her family. He said he needed a distraction," Sam said.

"You know about the money?"

She nodded. "The money wasn't a part of the hit. One of the guards was his target. He said the money was for his retirement."

"I don't suppose he said where he stashed it?" Andrea asked.

"No."

"He killed his team," Tori said. "There were three guys with him."

"Actually, there were four others," Sam said. "Three guys went in with him. He had another guy waiting at the car where they transferred the money." She looked over at Cameron. "Two of the guys were ex-military. He said they tried to take the money for themselves so he killed them."

"Their bodies were found south of Taos," Cameron said. "We only knew about three men. Are you saying there's another guy out there?"

Sam shook her head. "No. He said he killed them all. He said they were behind schedule and there were cops everywhere. He said he needed a distraction, but I got the impression that he intended on eliminating his team all along. He didn't go into details though. I assumed the distraction was the family."

Cameron shook her head. "There was a multicar accident on the highway. Some of the drivers had been shot. One was recognized as the fourth member of his team. He killed the family when the sheriff's department was all out investigating the accident."

"Which is why Tori and Casey were called to that scene," Sam said.

"Yeah."

"Well, he didn't—"

But Cameron's phone interrupted and she held her hand up to Sam. It was Murdock. She stood quickly. "Excuse me. It's the boss." She walked into the bedroom, giving herself some privacy. She'd talked at length with him earlier and was surprised he'd called back. "Ross. What's up?" she asked as Lola squeezed through the door before she could close it.

"How's the debriefing going?"

"It's going," she said. "Samantha seems very forthcoming with information, but we're just getting started."

"Well, I guess you can stop. They picked up Angel about a half hour ago."

"Are you kidding me? They found him? Where?"

"They're holding him in Taos. He drove right into a checkpoint, if you can believe that. At Angel Fire Resort. Kinda ironic, don't you think?"

Cameron shook her head. "He's smarter than that, Murdock. He could recognize a checkpoint."

"You'd think, right? Reports are they roughed him up pretty good though."

"Can't blame them. He's left bodies all over the county."

"Yes, I know." Murdock paused. "He offered up a proposition."

"Is he in a position to do that?"

"He's got three million dollars hidden somewhere. He's offered to give up the location."

"For?"

"He wants to see Kennedy."

"What the hell, Murdock? I'm sure Sam doesn't want any part of that deal."

"He'll be locked in a cell. She'll be safe. He wants a brief chat with her, that's all. Then they'll transport him back to Santa Fe."

"They know how dangerous he is, right? How are they handling the transport?"

"Federal marshals. They've thanked us for our assistance, but it's their deal now. From Santa Fe to Taos and nearly all the way to Eagle Nest, Angel's left carnage behind. I fear that if he even looks at one of them wrong they'll put a bullet in his head," Murdock said bluntly. "They're going to send in a couple of our agents from the Albuquerque office to deal with the three million," he said. "Talk with Kennedy. They want to do it first thing in the morning."

"Okay, I'll tell her. But if it was me, I'd tell him to go fuck himself."

Murdock laughed. "I'm sure you would. But three million is three million. Recovering that is a priority."

"So she talks to him, they take him to Santa Fe, then our job here is done? We can head out?"

"Your job is done. And I'm sure Agent Hunter and Kennedy are more than ready to head back to Dallas."

"Sounds like a plan," she said. "Andrea and I will head back to Colorado then. Unless you've got something else lined up?" She sat on the edge of the bed and let Lola climb into her lap.

"No. You guys did a great job on this. You deserve a break. I'll hold off on an assignment for at least a couple of weeks."

"Thanks, Murdock. I don't mind saying, I'm getting too damn old for chasing lunatics through the mountains on foot."

"Well, if you wanted to chat with that lunatic tomorrow too, feel free. Angel might as well know who it was chasing him."

Cameron smiled. "That I might do."

He disconnected without another word, and she slipped her phone back into her pocket. Lola was curled in her lap, her loud purring vibrating against her leg. Cameron took a few seconds to rub her chin, then nudged her off. She didn't know what Sam's feelings would be about the proposition, but Cameron was ready to get it over with. As soon as Angel was on his way to Santa Fe, she planned to hit the road back to Colorado.

She went out into the living room and found them chatting about Patrick Doe, of all things. She arched an eyebrow and Andrea smiled.

"I was telling them how we caught Patrick," she explained.

"I especially liked the part where you jumped off a cliff and nearly landed on a cactus," Tori said with a laugh.

"Very funny," Cameron said. "I damn near broke my ankle." She sat back down in her recliner and took a swallow of her now warm beer. "Got some news," she said. "They found Angel."

Sam leaned forward. "They caught him?"

"Yeah. At a checkpoint near Angel Fire Resort. They're going to take him back to Santa Fe in the morning. But before he'll give up the location of the money, he wanted to...to see you," she said to Sam.

"See me?"

"Murdock said Angel's proposition was that in exchange for the money, he wanted a chat with you."

"No way," Tori said. "She's been through enough, Cameron. There's no reason she—"

"There's a three million dollar reason," Cameron said bluntly.

"What...what does he want?" Sam asked.

Cameron shrugged. "Don't know. They're holding him in Taos. He'll be in a cell. It's not like you'd talk to him in an interrogation room or anything."

"I don't like it," Tori said.

Sam glanced at her and nodded. "I know you don't." She turned to Cameron. "But I'll do it."

CHAPTER TWENTY-TWO

Sam stared down the long corridor, trying to make sense of her feelings. Angel had violently hit Leslie, to the point of knocking her unconscious. He had killed that innocent family. He had killed so many that day. And he had abducted her at gunpoint. Tied her hands with a rope, threatened to kill her. She had been frightened, yes. But from the very beginning, from the moment she'd looked into his eyes, she'd seen something... something she couldn't put her finger on. She thought, maybe, subconsciously, she'd known all along that he wouldn't kill her.

"Ma'am?"

Sam turned to the young guard who stood beside her. She offered him a quick smile. "I'm fine."

"I'll take you down there."

"No need," she said. "I can manage."

"No offense, ma'am, but he's one mean son of a bitch," he said.

Sam squared her shoulders. "And no offense to you, but I do this for a living."

He raised his eyebrows.

"Dallas Police Department," she said.

"You're a cop?"

"Yes."

He looked past her, down the row of empty cells. "I should still go with you. They—"

"You can wait here if you want," she said, taking a step away from him. "He wanted to see me, not you."

She left the guard standing where he was as she headed down to the last cell. To say she'd been shocked that Angel had been caught so quickly was an understatement. He'd gone to such lengths to escape, to stay hidden. They'd walked for days across the mountains to avoid the highway. Why had he gotten caught? Cameron questioned it as well. Tori and Andrea didn't know Angel. Not that Sam could say she knew him well, not like Cameron. But from what she did know, he was smarter than to drive right up to a checkpoint.

"Sam? Is that you?"

She smiled when she heard his voice. "Yes."

She walked closer, stopping at his cell. It was dark and he was sitting in the shadows. When he stood, she heard the rustle of chains. He was wearing an orange jumpsuit and his legs were shackled—leg irons. He came into the light and she gasped. His lip was split open, one of his eyes was discolored and badly swollen.

"Yeah, they had a little fun with me," he said.

"I'm sorry," she whispered.

He shrugged, and she noticed that his hands were cuffed as well. "At least they didn't shoot me."

She met his gaze through the bars. "Why did you get caught, Angel?"

"Why? It wasn't like it was intentional."

"Wasn't it?"

He stared at her for a long moment, then his good eye wrinkled up in a smile. "So you made it out okay? No mountain lions?"

She smiled too. "No mountain lions. Actually, they were only about two hours behind us."

"Oh yeah? Your Tori?"

Sam nodded.

"I guess your faith in her paid off." He looked past her. "Am I going to meet her?"

Sam shook her head. "I don't think that's a good idea. She wants to shoot you."

Angel laughed, then winced and brought his hand up to his busted lip. "Damn," he murmured. Then, "She wants to shoot me, huh? She'll have to get in line."

"I imagine." She took a step closer to the bars. "Is this what…what this is about? What if I hadn't made it out okay?" she asked.

He shrugged. "I guess I would have led them to where I left you." He looked away. "I had to make sure you were okay, Sam."

"So you're trading a visit with me for three million dollars?"

"Yeah. What? You don't think you're worth that much?"

"When there were no helicopters searching for us, you didn't think I was," she reminded him.

"Well, I know they wanted the money. And I wanted to…to make sure you were back in civilization," he said. "It seemed like a fair exchange."

"Thank you for being worried about me," she said quietly. She looked down, then back to him. "I'm having a hard time with all of this, Angel," she admitted.

"What do you mean?"

"I mean, I know who you are, what you did. Yet I'm having a hard time separating all that from the man I came to know."

"Sam, I'm still the man who abducted you. I held a goddamn gun to your head," he said, his voice cracking. "And I'm so, so sorry for that."

"Why, Angel? Why are you sorry? Isn't that who you are?"

Their gazes locked together for a long instance. He nodded. "Yes. Yes, that's who I am, Sam. Don't forget it. But you…you were…you were different."

"Different?"

"You cared."

She nodded. "Maybe that's what has got me so shaken," she said.

"Because I'm a killer?"

"Yes. And now, there's absolutely nothing I can do for you."

"Believe it or not, I've been in worse jams than this," he said, holding his cuffed hands up.

Sam turned when she heard the far cell door open to the corridor. "Looks like...my time is up," she said quietly. She heard footsteps approaching.

"Yeah, I guess." He brought his hands up, wrapping his fingers around the bars. "You take care of yourself, Sam."

She reached out and touched one of his hands gently, her gaze locked with his. "I will." She took a deep breath. She had no words of comfort for him. He would spend the rest of his life in prison. "Goodbye, Angel."

She turned and was surprised to find Cameron waiting for her. She looked at her questioningly.

"I wanted a quick word with him," Cameron explained.

Sam nodded then walked past her, turning once, seeing Angel's hands still clutching the bars.

* * *

Cameron stopped in front of Angel, seeing shock and recognition on his bruised face.

"Damn. Cameron Ross. Now there's a name from the past." He looked her over. "What the hell are you doing here?"

She tilted her head a bit. "FBI," she said easily.

He laughed. "FBI? Figures." He met her gaze. "Let me guess. You were the one tracking me?"

She nodded. "You did a pretty good job. The rain on that last night set me back a bit."

"I'm sure it did." He glanced away, then back to her. "So Sam...you know her?"

"No. Just met."

"You met her partner? Tori?"

"Yeah. She was on the mission with me."

"What's she like?"

Cameron frowned, wondering at his question. She hadn't seen Angel in a number of years, but she remembered him as cold, impersonal. But his question seemed genuine.

"Arrogant," she said. "Kinda bossy. Thinks she knows everything."

He smiled. "Hell, sounds like you're describing yourself there, Ross."

Cameron smiled, then slowly shook her head. "Angel, what the hell happened to you? You were a good soldier once. Why all this?"

"Why not? The military taught me to kill. I was good at it." He paused. "So were you."

"I simply did my job, nothing more," she said.

"Yeah? Well, when I got out, there was no cushy FBI job waiting for me," he said. "But there were other governments willing to pay for my talents. Governments and opposition leaders, both."

"Using your talents in a war zone is one thing. Coming over here, killing innocent people is quite another. Killing that family…"

"Yeah, well, that was unfortunate."

She shoved her hands into her pockets. "That's it? Unfortunate?" She shook her head. "Angel, you're damn lucky New Mexico repealed their death penalty."

"Am I?"

She recognized the indifference in his voice and knew he had no remorse whatsoever. She turned to go, then stopped. "Why a hostage, Angel? Doesn't really seem your style."

He shrugged. "Seemed like a good idea at the time. I was working on Plan C, since A and B were fucked," he said.

"And after all of that, you get sloppy and drive into a checkpoint?"

He moved away from the bars, into the shadows. "Yeah, well, it had been a really long week."

She had not worked with Angel in several years, but the man who was on her team was always meticulous, never sloppy. She was about to question him further, but the loud clanging of the cell doors down the corridor stopped her. She heard several footsteps approaching and she stepped back. She doubted he would have anything else to say.

CHAPTER TWENTY-THREE

The drive back to the campground was made in relative silence. Andrea glanced out of the corner of her eye, seeing Tori and Sam holding hands in the backseat. She looked at Cameron, who appeared deep in thought. Cameron had said little since they'd left. Sam had said even less. She turned around in her seat, meeting Tori's gaze. It was as questioning as her own.

"So, are we just not going to talk about it?" she finally asked, looking first at Cameron, then Sam.

"What's to talk about?" Cameron asked.

"Oh, how about the fact that we've been chasing this bastard through the goddamn woods for days," Tori said, "and neither of you are saying a thing about it."

"I told you, he wanted to see if I'd made it out okay," Sam said.

"That's it?"

"Yes, Tori, that's it."

Andrea glanced at Cameron. "And you?"

"Me? I told him he was getting sloppy in his old age," Cameron said. Cameron glanced in the rearview mirror. "Did he say anything about the checkpoint?"

Sam shook her head. "I asked him why he got caught," she said. "He said it wasn't intentional, but I think it was."

Cameron nodded. "So do I."

"What do you mean?" Tori asked.

"The Angel I know could spot a checkpoint a mile away. Hell, we had to avoid checkpoints all the damn time," Cameron said. "Nothing about this feels right."

"Maybe he was tired of running," Andrea suggested. "Maybe he knew there would be no way out."

"So he turns himself in?" Cameron shook her head. "He'd just gone on a killing rampage because he didn't want to get caught. We're trained *not* to get caught," she said.

"So what are you thinking?" Tori asked.

"I don't know. It makes no damn sense. So they take him back to Santa Fe and he tells them where the money is. Makes no difference. He's still going to rot in prison. There's nothing in it for him," Cameron said. "And that's what the problem is. It's all too easy. There's got to be something more to it."

"Maybe he's genuinely sorry for what he did," Sam said.

"No," Cameron said. "That's not his style."

"People change."

"Not Angel."

Sam didn't say anything else, and neither did Cameron. Andrea glanced again at Tori, who only let out a heavy sigh. The silence was again loud in the truck, and Andrea searched for a topic to break it.

"You two are heading back to Texas in the morning?"

Sam didn't acknowledge the question, but Tori nodded. "Yeah. Renting a car. What about you?"

"I guess we'll head back to Colorado until our next assignment," she said.

Cameron simply nodded but said nothing. Andrea sighed, giving up on conversation. She turned her attention to the road as Cameron made the drive from Taos back to their campground.

* * *

Tori dug through the bag that Casey had left them for some clean jeans. The sun was shining brightly, but it was a cool afternoon. And for the rest of the day, they were going to pretend they were still on vacation. Andrea had offered to cook an early dinner for the four of them, and Cameron had let them have her truck. She glanced to where Sam stood, her back to her. Sam had spoken to Leslie earlier. She'd been extremely quiet ever since.

"You okay?" she asked for the fourth time. Sam had already changed and was standing at the window looking out.

Sam turned to her, offering a quick smile. "Yes, Tori. I'm fine."

It was the same answer she'd given the other three times. She tossed the jeans down and walked over to her. "Why won't you talk to me?"

Sam leaned closer, letting their shoulders touch. "I'm simply trying to make sense of it, Tori." She turned then, meeting her eyes. "I'm a cop. He's a killer. Yet we have this connection between us. I can't explain it."

"Like…like an attraction?" she asked hesitantly.

Sam gave a quick laugh. "God, no. Is that what you think?"

"I don't know what to think," she admitted. "I haven't met the guy." She ran a hand through her dark hair in frustration. "I just—"

"I know. You're worried about me."

Tori met her gaze. "Yes. I feel like he's gotten inside your head."

Sam nodded. "Yes. Yes, he has."

"Sam…he's a killer. He's—"

"I know, Tori. Don't you think I know all of that?"

Tori let out a breath. "I'm sorry. I'm trying—"

"I can deal with this." Sam leaned closer and kissed her. "I love you, Tori. More than anything in this whole world. Don't ever doubt that."

Tori closed her eyes for a moment, enjoying the closeness as Sam kissed her again.

"I know. I love you too."

"Now, I bet there's a beer calling your name," Sam said. "I think sitting outside in the sunshine will be just the ticket." She stepped away from Tori. "Besides, I'm looking forward to getting to know them better. Andrea seems very likable. Cameron has an edge to her."

"Yeah, I told you, arrogant and bossy."

Sam grinned. "Maybe that's why I like her. She reminds me of you."

CHAPTER TWENTY-FOUR

Cameron had just opened a beer and sat down in the lawn chair when she saw a flash of their truck through the trees. She turned back to the opened door of the motorhome. "They're here," she called.

"Try to be nice," Andrea said from the doorway.

Cameron smiled. "Me?"

"Yes, you. I know you have questions for Sam, but let it go. It's over with."

Cameron nodded. Yes, she had questions. But it didn't really matter any longer. Angel was in custody. Tori and Sam would be heading back to Dallas, and she and Andrea would head north to Colorado. Angel would already be back in Santa Fe by morning. Over and done with. But the nagging questions she had kept bouncing around in her head.

Something wasn't right. As she'd said, it was too easy. Angel wouldn't go down without a fight. Angel wouldn't simply drive up to a checkpoint and essentially turn himself in. There had to be a reason. Every move Angel made, there had to be a reason for it. And she wanted to get Sam off by herself, away from Tori and Andrea, and get her feelings on it. But really, she should do what Andrea said. Let it go. They would enjoy the rest of the day, visit a little, drink a few beers and share an early dinner. Then tomorrow, they would go their separate ways and chalk this up as another mission completed.

If only it were that easy.

"I hope we're not too early," Sam said as she got out of the truck.

"No. Right on time," Cameron said as she held up her beer. "First one."

Tori came out holding up a six-pack. "We stopped at that little grocery store. Didn't know what kind you drank, so I got what we like," she said as she pulled two from the pack, handing one to Sam.

Cameron stood and took the beer from her. "I'll put it in the fridge," she said. "Sit down."

"Does Andrea need help with anything?" Sam asked.

"No, we picked up some steaks. I think she's got potatoes in the oven," she said.

Andrea met her at the door and took the beer from her. "Go visit," she said. "I'll be out in a minute."

Cameron returned to her chair, her gaze going to first Tori, then Sam. There seemed to be a little tension between them. She wished Andrea would hurry. She'd never been good with small talk.

"So…hell of a vacation, huh?"

"Oh, yeah. Ranks right up there with the best," Tori said dryly, then turned to Sam. "Remind me to tell Casey 'no' the next time she invites us somewhere."

Sam smiled at her. "She was only trying to get us away from Dallas for a while," she said.

"Let's try the beach next time."

Cameron laughed with them. "Casey's partner, Leslie…I guess she recovered okay?"

Sam nodded. "Yes. I talked to Leslie earlier. She seems fine. She's going to take a few days off before she goes back to work though."

"Good." Cameron looked over at Tori. "Why FBI?" Tori raised her eyebrows and Cameron clarified. "Your best friends are with Homicide. You were a detective there too. You don't seem FBI material."

Sam laughed at that, and Tori scowled at Cameron. "Oh? And like you are?"

"No offense," Cameron said. "Just…you don't appear to put up with bullshit." Cameron glanced up as Andrea joined them. "I don't either. If I was stuck in an office having to follow goddamn protocol all the time, I'd shoot myself."

Tori nodded. "Yeah, I hate that part of it." She looked over at Sam. "Actually, I hate pretty much all of it."

"You do?" Sam asked. "I thought you loved it."

"No. It was a change I needed at the time, that's all. Like Cameron said, bullshit and politics."

"A large police force like Dallas, you wouldn't think it would be much different," Andrea said as she joined the conversation. "I used to work for LAPD. I remember well the bullshit and politics there."

"There's some, yeah," Tori said. "But for the most part, our lieutenant dealt with that." Tori looked at Sam. "I miss it. I miss the team."

Sam reached over and grabbed her hand. "So go back."

Tori nodded. "Yeah, I've been thinking about it."

Cameron watched as their eyes met, and she saw a gentle look pass between them.

"I think that would be wonderful," Sam said as she squeezed her hand again. "Casey would love it." Then Sam laughed. "I wonder how much trouble you two could get into."

"Tori told me that you and she started out as partners on the force," Andrea said.

"We did." Sam nodded. "She was mean and bossy, and I'm pretty sure I called her a bully at some point."

Andrea laughed. "I called Cameron a bully too. Among other things."

Cameron looked at Tori with raised eyebrows. "Do you have any idea what they're talking about?"

"Not a clue," Tori said with a shake of her head.

"Tori hated partners," Sam continued. "I think she was trying to run me off."

Cameron's phone interrupted their conversation, and she glanced at Andrea. "Murdock again? I thought he was going to spare us for a while." She stood and pulled her phone out of her pocket. "Excuse me," she said to Tori and Sam as she walked away before answering.

"Are you on the road yet?" he asked.

"No. Actually, we have company," she said, tossing a quick glance over her shoulder. "Andrea thought an early dinner with Agent Hunter and Kennedy would be appropriate," she said. "They're heading out tomorrow too."

He sighed. "Change of plans," he said, and she recognized the weariness in his voice.

"What's up?"

"Angel."

Cameron frowned. "What about him?"

"He escaped. Took out eight goddamn men."

"What the hell?"

"They were on their way to Santa Fe. Four marshals in a sheriff's department van with him. Two deputies and our two agents were following behind in an unmarked car. They radioed in that they were stopping. They were on Highway 285," he said.

"Why stopping?"

"He was taking them to the location of the money. That's the last communication. When they didn't show in Santa Fe, well…"

"Are you kidding me?"

"I wish I was. This all went down about two hours ago," he said. "Details are still coming in."

Cameron ran a hand through her hair, then looked over at their guests. They were still chatting with Andrea. "So we're back on the case?"

"I don't know who the hell has jurisdiction right now," Murdock said. "Sheriff's departments in two different counties are working it, U.S. marshals are working it. I've got orders to send a team back in. It's not going to be pretty. Too many agencies have a stake in it now. We're going to be tripping all over ourselves," he said.

"So cooperation will be at a minimum? What about the Albuquerque office?"

"It's personal for them now too, but they've been told to back off. He's ex-military. You've got a history with him. You've been on the case since the beginning. I'm trying to pull some strings so you can take the lead on this, but hell, Cameron, you know how it is. The locals want their hand in it too."

"In other words, Angel won't be taken alive," she said.

"Not if they get to him before we do."

"Is that such a bad thing, Murdock? How many has he killed?"

"Too damn many. They're running his photo all over the news, they tell me. You'll have people seeing him in every corner, every store, every damn gas station," he said.

"Okay. Well, let me break up our dinner party. And I was looking forward to steaks too," she said.

"Sorry," he said. "Get out to the scene as soon as you can. Not sure what you could find that hasn't already been gone over. The rest of your team is coming in tonight."

She frowned. "What team?"

"Reynolds."

"Reynolds? What the hell are you bringing in Reynolds for?"

"Because he's got a computer geek that you can use and he and his team are in between assignments." He paused. "Besides, one of the agents that was killed—Humphrey—he and Reynolds have a history."

"And you think that's a good thing?"

"Sometimes when things are personal, there's a little more urgency."

Cameron frowned. "Are you suggesting that I wasn't urgent enough on this?"

"I'm suggesting no such thing, Agent Ross. I'm disappointed we didn't get our hands on him before the locals did, that's all. And what's wrong with Reynolds? I thought you and he worked great together out in the desert."

"After I got him to loosen up a little, yeah. But I know how to use my goddamn computers, Murdock. I really don't need Reynolds and his team on this."

"I need you out in the field, Cameron. Let Rowan do his thing on the computers. Oh, and brief Agent Hunter. She stays on with you too."

Cameron walked around the side of the motorhome, shaking her head. "No way. We don't get along well enough for this. She's…temperamental," she said. "I don't need her."

"You might. Reynolds' team is thin, just Eric and Rowan. With Rowan's nose buried in your computers, you might need another body. Hunter stays on. I've already cleared it." He laughed lightly. "Try to play nice with everybody, Cameron."

"Yeah, yeah. And what about Kennedy?"

"Before you cut her loose, make sure you get everything you need from her regarding Angel. Reynolds and his team are on their way. They'll meet you in Taos. You can decide if you want to move your operation to Santa Fe or not. Check your email. I'll send all the specifics."

He disconnected before she could protest any further, and she blew out her breath before pocketing her phone. Great. Just great. Stuck here again with Hunter.

She walked back around to where the others were. Andrea's eyes flew to hers, eyebrows raised.

"Yeah," she said. "Change of plans." She looked at Sam. "Angel has escaped."

Sam's eyebrows shot up in surprise, but it was Tori who spoke.

"That son of a bitch," Tori murmured.

"Yeah. Murdock says you're to stay and work this with us."

Tori let out a long breath. "Great," she said dryly.

"Yeah. That was pretty much my sentiment too."

CHAPTER TWENTY-FIVE

Sam stood back, feeling in the way as everyone jostled around her. Andrea was talking to two federal marshals and Tori and Cameron were walking outside the perimeter of the crime scene tape, looking for tracks, Tori had said. She turned away, heading back to Cameron's truck. Cameron had emailed her a file that Murdock had put together on Angel. Cameron wanted her to see if there was anything she could add to it, based on the conversations she'd had with him.

She shook her head. She couldn't believe that he had escaped, that he had killed eight men in doing so. Eight law enforcement personnel. They didn't know the details yet, didn't know how he managed that. But she knew without Cameron having to tell her that if Angel was spotted, he wouldn't be taken into custody. No. Not this time. Unspoken orders, but orders nonetheless—shoot to kill. Angel would not walk out of this one alive.

Cameron had said that Angel was good. That he was very, very good. Had they let their guard down with him? Did they underestimate him? Something that he'd said to her that very morning stuck out. He said he'd been in worse jams than this one. Had he been planning his escape all along? But why would he get caught in the first place? Why drive into a checkpoint? It had to be intentional, which made no sense at all. Unless it was as he'd said, he wanted to make sure Sam had made it out okay. Was that it? Had he simply been worried about her enough to get caught, knowing he could escape at will?

No. No one could possibly be that confident.

She looked around, past the activity, into the forest that bordered the dirt road they were on. Was he out there somewhere? Had he taken to the woods again? Or was he on the road, running? He'd left all eight bodies inside the van and had taken the car. He'd removed his shackles and changed clothes, leaving the orange jumpsuit behind and taking the clothes from one of the FBI agents, right down to the shoes. Shoes and credentials and his service weapon.

She got in the front seat on the passenger's side but left the door open. She and Tori were taking the truck. Cameron and Andrea's motorhome was parked up on the highway. They would be heading back to Taos as soon as they were through here. She and Tori would stay in a hotel, the same one where Cameron's new team was going to stay. Murdock had already arranged that, and Andrea had secured a campground only a few miles away. The shadows were long with the sun nearly gone from the sky. She sighed and got out her phone, pulling up Cameron's email. She wasn't sure how much help she could be, but she would read through the report.

It was in a timeline format which was easy to follow, but it wasn't very detailed. They knew he had lived in the Taos area as a kid, she saw. The report made note of his mother's death in California but no mention that his father had been drinking at the time of the accident. It covered his military years and when he got out, nearly six years ago now. She noticed there was a break in time, right after he got out. Two years were missing before it picked back up, with Angel back in the Middle East.

But even then, there were gaps in the timeline. According to this, he got back in the States just six months ago. Nothing after that.

"Well?"

She looked up, startled to find Cameron standing beside the truck watching her. She shook her head. "There's not much here."

"No. They didn't have a whole lot of time to put this together. Bare bones," she said. "But he's kept a low profile. When we were on assignment, we had to learn to disappear from time to time. Go under the radar. He's good at it."

"He told me his father was a drinker, that he was drunk when he had the accident that killed his mother." Sam shrugged. "I know, it doesn't help any with all of this."

"Did you know he'd lived here?"

Sam nodded. "Yes. He said they moved to California when he was twelve. The route that he took us on through the mountains was planned through research though. Not from what he remembered as a child." She looked past Cameron to where Tori and Andrea were chatting. It was nearly dark now, and she couldn't make out their expressions. "There are gaps. I guess like you said, when he was under the radar. But two years are missing," she said.

"Yeah. After he got out of the military. He disappeared," Cameron said. "Murdock said there were no hits on him anywhere during that time."

"What do you think?" she asked.

Cameron shrugged. "He could have still been working. Using an alias," she said.

"Then he resurfaced using his own name? Why?"

Cameron shrugged again. "I'm only guessing, Sam, nothing more."

Sam shook her head quickly. "He didn't seem the type to use an alias," she said. "He seemed almost proud of his accomplishments, both in the military and beyond. That type of person would want the recognition, not be anonymous."

"True. But what other explanation could there be?"

Sam pictured Angel's face, seeing the smile, the relaxed look he'd sported when they'd been fishing. He wasn't a killer then. He was…he was almost a friend. She looked at Cameron. "Maybe he wasn't working then. Maybe for those two years, he was just a normal guy."

"Where? Murdock said they could find nothing on him. His military pension's been going into an account he set up, but it hasn't been touched at all."

"You were in his unit, on his team. I imagine the assignments you had, it must have taken its toll on you. When you got out, what did you do?"

Cameron stared at her for the longest time, and she thought perhaps she wasn't going to answer her. Cameron finally sighed.

"I didn't exactly retire, Sam. Not like Angel. I was too young for that. But I was burned out. I couldn't do it anymore. You're right. It took its toll and I was ready to walk away, leave it behind. We reached a compromise," she said.

"With Murdock?"

"Not at first, no. I was on a team of four. But I was told I didn't play nice with others," Cameron said with a quick smile. "The motorhome, that was an experimental assignment only. I traveled alone. It suited me."

"Until you met Andrea?"

Cameron nodded but said nothing else.

"So…it's not experimental any longer?" Sam knew the question could apply to either the motorhome or Andrea. Cameron's quick smile told her she understood the double question.

"No. It's not experimental any longer."

Sam would have asked more questions, but Tori and Andrea walked over.

"Ready to head out?" Andrea asked. "I got a text from Eric. They flew in to Albuquerque earlier," she said. "Got briefed there. They're on the road now, heading this way. About forty-five minutes out."

"Okay. I guess we need to get back to Taos and set up camp," Cameron said. "Meet for a working dinner? Don't know about you guys, but I'm starving."

"There'll be seven of us?" Tori asked. "Kinda hard to have a working dinner, isn't it?"

"Not if we order pizza and eat it in your hotel room," Cameron said with a wink at Andrea.

"How did I know that would be your suggestion?" Andrea glanced at Sam. "Did I mention she's obsessed with pizza?"

CHAPTER TWENTY-SIX

Andrea laughed good-naturedly as Eric drew her into a hug, kissing her quickly on the mouth. "You're as beautiful as I remembered," he said.

"And you're as charming as I remembered," she said. She ran a hand playfully through his hair. "You and long hair? It was nearly military short the last time I saw you."

"Yeah, I wanted a change," he said as he brushed it away from his face. "Besides, Reynolds hates it. Annoying him is the only fun I have these days."

Cameron walked over to them. "No kissing," she said with barely a hint of a smile.

"I'm not scared of you," he said with a grin. Then he took Cameron's offered hand, shaking it briskly. "Good to see you again, Agent Ross."

"Yeah, you too. Where's Reynolds?"

"Still in his room, I guess. He takes longer to get dressed than me," he said, motioning to his jeans and T-shirt. "And

Rowan had his nose stuck in his computer." Eric turned to Sam and Tori and gave them an easy smile. "I'm Eric Scales."

Tori held her hand out first. "Tori Hunter, FBI, Dallas." She motioned to Sam. "This is Sam Kennedy, Dallas PD."

Eric nodded. "You were the hostage."

"Yes."

"From everything we learned about this guy, you're damn lucky," he said bluntly.

Sam simply nodded but didn't comment.

"So all of you have worked together before?" Tori asked.

"Yes. Serial killer," Andrea said. "California desert." She glanced at Eric. "So where did Murdock pull you from?"

"We were in Nevada. Had a kidnapping." He shook his head. "It didn't end well."

"So how is Reynolds?" Cameron asked. "He still doing everything by the book?"

"Oh, he's loosened up a little. Very little."

"He still insist on wearing suits and ties? I know when we last saw you, he was dressing down a bit."

"Yeah, he likes his suits, that's for sure. But he's not quite as fanatical about it," Eric said. "In fact, tonight, I bet he wears only a starched shirt."

Cameron grinned. "I'll bet you ten bucks he has on a tie."

Eric shook his head. "No way. He knows you. He also knows we're having pizza brought in for dinner."

"Ten bucks."

"You're on."

Andrea turned to Tori and Sam. "When we were in the desert, Reynolds had on a suit and tie, dress shoes, the works," she explained. "He and Cameron disagreed on the dress code."

"Yes, Tori's had her run-in with the dress code too," Sam said with a smile.

"Another reason to go back to Homicide," Tori said.

Cameron glanced at her. "So pizza is ordered, right?"

Andrea nodded. "On its way."

They were in Tori and Sam's hotel room and it was already a little crowded. Cameron pulled out the lone chair and sat down, stretching her long legs out. Tori and Sam sat on one of the beds and Eric sat down on the other. A quick knock on the door and Tori got up, opening it. Reynolds stood there, his ebony skin in dark contrast against the white of his starched shirt. A red tie dangled from his neck, and Andrea glanced over at Cameron who was smiling.

"Nice tie, Reynolds," Cameron said with a smirk, holding out her hand to Eric. He slapped a ten-dollar bill there. "Thank you very much," Cameron said.

Reynolds stared at Eric disapprovingly as he walked into the room. He was followed closely by Rowan, his laptop tucked under one arm.

"Very Special Agent Ross, so good to see you again," Reynolds said. He turned toward her. "Andrea, you're looking well."

She smiled at him. "Thank you." She pointed at Tori and Sam. "This is Tori Hunter, she's from the Dallas office. And Sam Kennedy, Dallas PD," Andrea introduced. "This is Special Agent Reynolds."

Reynolds nodded as he shook their hands. "Hell of an ordeal you had."

"And apparently it's not over," Tori said.

Cameron stood, walking over to shake Reynolds's hand as well. "What's with the tie? I thought you'd loosened up a little," she said.

"Well, it's a business meeting," he said. "And we have guests."

"It's pizza," Cameron clarified. "And Tori and Sam are no longer guests." She turned to Rowan. "How the hell are you?"

Rowan gave her a quick smile. "Good. I understand I'm going to get to play with your computers again."

"So Murdock tells me," Cameron said. She pointed at him. "We'll go over some ground rules first."

"You know, Jason and I are pretty good buds now," Rowan said.

"Is that right? Have you been stalking him?"

Rowan blushed. "Well, maybe a little."

Andrea laughed, remembering the near infatuation Rowan had with Jason, Cameron's computer guru.

Another knock on the door signaled the arrival of the pizza and it was a whirlwind of activity as they all passed around boxes, piling their plates high. All but Sam, Andrea noticed. She took only one piece. Andrea sat down on one of the beds next to Eric. Cameron leaned against the dresser as Reynolds took the chair she'd been in earlier.

"We haven't eaten since lunch," Eric said around a bite.

"At least you had lunch," Cameron said. "Oh, God," she murmured as she bit into her piece. "That's so good."

Reynolds wiped his mouth with a napkin before speaking. "I understand you and Angel served together," he said. "How well do you know him?"

"We were on the same team for a few years," Cameron said. "He was very good. You could trust him to do his job and not screw it up." She shrugged. "But personally, I wouldn't say I knew him well. He kept to himself, didn't talk a lot. He just did his job."

"I imagine he's older than you are."

Cameron nodded. "Late forties now, I guess." She glanced over at Sam. "Wouldn't you agree?"

"Yes."

Reynolds turned his attention to Sam. "I'm told you met with him in his cell. What was discussed?"

Sam shifted uncomfortably under Reynolds's stare, Andrea noticed. She also noted that Sam had eaten very little of the one piece of pizza she had claimed. She didn't know Sam at all, but she sensed a war going on inside of her. Their debriefing of her had been superficial at best. When Murdock had called to say Angel had been apprehended, they'd pretty much stopped with the questions. Angel was in custody and their job was done. That, of course, turned out to be short-lived.

"We really didn't discuss much of anything," Sam said to Reynolds.

"He merely requested your presence...for what then?"

"He said he wanted to make sure I'd gotten off the mountain safely," Sam said quietly. "That's about it."

"Look, what does that have to do with anything?" Tori asked. "So he wanted to see her? Maybe he was feeling guilty for having abducted her in the first place."

"Not his style," Cameron said. "There is no guilt."

"Did he ask you any questions? Did he ask for a favor?" Reynolds continued. "Did he mention his plans?"

At that, Sam gave a humorless laugh. "Yeah, he told me he planned to escape. Told me how he was going to do it, too. I just thought I'd keep that to myself, though. No sense in giving anyone a heads-up, right?"

Andrea and Cameron exchanged glances, then Cameron walked between Reynolds and Sam to get another piece of pizza from the table.

"Don't patronize her, Reynolds," Cameron mumbled as she stuffed half the piece in her mouth.

"I'm just—"

"Being a dick." Cameron sat down next to Tori on the bed. "The latest from Murdock is that this is still a joint effort with the locals and the U.S. Marshals Service. They've got Angel's picture posted all over the damn place. We all know the problem with that. They're getting calls from everywhere. They'll be chasing shadows all over the state," she said. "The sheriff's department has limited resources. I don't think they'll get close to finding Angel. The Marshals Service is the best at locating fugitives, or so they keep telling us," she said with a quick grin. "But they don't have Rowan."

Rowan looked up as his name was spoken. His laptop was balanced on one thigh and a plate with pizza on the other.

"What do you want me to do?"

Cameron shrugged. "Simple. Find him."

Rowan looked nervously at Reynolds. The last time they'd worked together, Cameron had Rowan hacking into systems he had no business being in. It had been a bone of contention between Reynolds and Cameron.

"By the book," Reynolds stated.

"By whatever means necessary," Cameron countered. "To quote Murdock," she added. Cameron glanced back at Rowan. "Angel is not on the run. Not yet."

"How can you be sure?" Eric asked.

"Because the point of this whole operation of his was to get three million dollars. We find where he stashed the money, we find him."

"Provided he hasn't already snatched it up and fled," Tori said.

"Doubtful," Cameron said. "There's law enforcement crawling all over the place.

Reynolds shook his head. "I don't agree with you," he said. "At our briefing, we were led to believe that Angel Figueroa was a hit man. He has just killed two of our FBI agents. He killed four federal marshals. He killed two deputies. All in order to escape. No way he hangs around waiting for a chance to claim the money. I think he's long gone from this area."

Before Cameron could speak, Sam beat her to it.

"You're wrong, Agent Reynolds. It was always about the money," Sam said. "Cameron is right. Find the money, we find him."

Reynolds narrowed his eyes at her. "So he did share some things with you after all. I suspected as much."

It was Tori who protested this time. "Why the hell are you treating Sam as a goddamn suspect?" she demanded. "She was the one who was abducted."

Reynolds raised his hands. "Hey, I'm simply trying to get caught up on everything," he said. "I've worked with Cameron before. She tends to gloss over things if they don't suit her."

Cameron laughed. "Oh, now come on, Reynolds. Are you going all the way back to when you were on Collie's team? I thought we were past that."

Andrea leaned closer to Eric. "I thought you said he'd mellowed," she whispered.

He grinned. "Apparently not with Cameron."

Reynolds put his plate on the table, his gaze still on Cameron. "I hear you never came close to Angel while you were tracking him. Is that true?"

Andrea's eyebrows rose as did Tori's. She couldn't imagine who Reynolds had heard that from. But the outburst she expected from Cameron never came. Instead, it was a rather lazy smile that Cameron gave him.

"I guess it depends on what you consider close," she said. "He had half a day's head start on us." She shrugged. "I thought we did pretty damn good."

"So did I," Sam said with a smile.

Cameron stood after a brief nod at Sam. "I don't think we're making much progress here. Do you?" she asked Reynolds.

"I'm assuming, just like out in the desert, you want me to hand over Rowan to you," he said.

Cameron shook her head. "What I want right now is for you and me to talk. How about we go to your room?"

Andrea watched Reynolds's face, surprised at the hostility there. When they'd parted company in Barstow, Reynolds had been friendly with Cameron. She couldn't imagine what had happened to change that.

"Very well. Perhaps we can come up with a plan of action."

The tension in the room was heavy, and Andrea and Eric exchanged glances. Reynolds opened the door and Cameron followed, closing it rather loudly behind her. Tori was the first to speak.

"What the hell was that all about?"

"I have no idea," Andrea said. She looked at Eric. "You?"

Eric nodded. "Yeah, I think I do. Apparently Cameron's being blamed for the two agents getting killed."

Andrea stood up quickly. "*What*? Why?"

"It's a bunch of crap, that's all," Eric said. "One of the agents killed was friends with Reynolds. Humphrey. They worked together years ago. When we got briefed in Albuquerque, well, they needed to place blame. Seems some think that since Cameron and Angel were on the same team in the military, she's got a soft spot for him or something. Reynolds went along with it."

"That's bullshit," Andrea said. "Cameron hasn't seen Angel in years. They weren't even close when they worked together." She clenched her fists angrily. "How about blaming the goddamn federal marshals who supposedly had him locked up in a van?"

"I didn't say I blamed her, Andi," Eric said. "I'm just telling you what the vibe is in Albuquerque."

Tori came and stood between them. "Okay, this isn't helping." She turned to Eric. "And for the record, we busted our ass out there trying to catch up with him. So, to quote Andrea, it's bullshit," she said. "Now, what are we going to do to find Angel?"

"Excuse me," Rowan said. "But I read through the file they put together on him. It's rather brief. I understand they didn't have a whole lot of time to dig." He glanced at Andrea. "It might be helpful if I tried to go a little deeper. Of course, using Cameron's supercomputers would be a lot quicker," he said as he tapped on his laptop. "But I've always been pretty good at removing layers to find out more." He looked up quickly. "Besides, Jason has given me some of his programs."

"Okay, yeah, that's a good idea." She turned to Sam. "And right now, Sam, you're the only one in this room who knows anything about him."

Sam nodded. "Yes." She looked at Rowan. "What do you need?"

* * *

Cameron slammed the door shut and stood facing Reynolds, hands on her hips. "What the hell is wrong with you?"

Reynolds took a step closer, pointing his finger at her. "Tell me what I'm hearing is not true," he said loudly.

"I don't know, man. What the hell are you hearing?"

"That you and Angel were friends. That you let him slip away on purpose."

"Jesus Christ, Reynolds. You don't actually believe that, do you?"

"I know the type of team you were on back then. I know the pressure—the stress—you were under. And I know how tight you become on a team like that. It's life or death. So if you and Angel were close, if you—"

"Come on, Reynolds." Cameron ran a hand through her hair. "I can't believe this," she murmured. "After all we went through in the Mojave Desert? After you and I chased that fucker Baskin at that goddamn waterpark?" She shook her head with a humorless laugh. "Really? You think I'd let a killer slip away because we were once on a Special Ops team together?"

"They said you—"

"They who?" she asked, interrupting him.

"Albuquerque."

"Oh. Of course. They lost two men."

"I lost…a friend," he said, his voice calmer now.

"And you need someone to blame," she guessed. "*They* need someone to blame."

Reynolds turned his back to her and let out a heavy breath. When he turned back around, she was surprised to see dampness in his eyes.

"Tell me the truth, Cameron. Tell me you did everything you possibly could to get that bastard."

"You know who the hostage was," she said. "And she and Agent Hunter…they're involved…romantically. Agent Hunter was with us as we tracked him. Maybe you should ask her if we did everything possible to catch him."

Reynolds let his shoulders sag. "I'd known Humphrey long before the FBI linked us. We met when we were nineteen. Hit it off right away. Stayed friends all these years," he said.

"I'm sorry," she said.

He nodded slowly. "Yeah. It was just such a shock."

"Our line of work," she said quietly.

"I know." He rubbed his face. "Hell, I know." He looked at her then. "I'm sorry, Cameron. You're right. I needed someone to blame."

Cameron tilted her head. "Murdock told me you knew Humphrey. So this case is personal for you."

"Yes."

She stared at him. "Remember at that bar in Needles? After we'd found Andrea? You told me when it gets personal, it gets dangerous. You said you let your emotions override your training."

He nodded. "Yes. I did say that. I was speaking of you and Andrea, of course. My relationship with Humphrey was very different than yours is with Andrea."

"Regardless, you're letting your emotions dictate your actions now. I know you and I don't have a lot of history," she said. "Your first impression of me was when you were with Collie. He was a bastard and he hated me."

"True."

"But after Barstow, after all that, I thought you trusted me." She took a step toward him. "Don't question my integrity, Reynolds. I don't always follow protocol, you know that. But I do my goddamn job." She shoved her hands in her pockets. "And for the record, Angel and I were never friends."

He met her gaze and didn't flinch. He only nodded.

"Okay," she said. "Then let's do our job now. Let's find this fucker."

CHAPTER TWENTY-SEVEN

"How did you find all this?"

Rowan shrugged. "It took me most of the night," he said. "He's been very careful."

"Have you emailed this to everyone?"

"No. Only you and Reynolds," he said.

"Okay. I'll forward it to my team," Cameron said. "I want Sam to read it." She smiled at him. "Good job, Rowan."

He blushed and shoved his glasses up higher on his nose.

"Come on back here," she said, leading him through the RV to the small computer room that housed four monitors and two different computers. "Nothing has changed since you were in here last." She glanced over her shoulder, looking for Reynolds. She could hear him talking to Andrea. "Actually, I don't use them as much as I should."

"Easier to call Jason?"

She laughed. "Yeah. Don't get me wrong. I can use most of the algorithms that he's written," she said. "But I don't always trust myself."

"That you're feeding the correct data, you mean?"

"Yeah. And that's the major problem here. We don't have much data to use. Not like in Barstow," she said. "You used the algorithms perfectly there. But with serial killers, we've got a lot of data to use. Patterns and whatnot."

Rowan had already pushed her out of the way and sat down. She smiled as he rubbed his hands together in anticipation. "If we need him, I've got Jason on speed dial," Rowan said.

"Good. Glad I'm not the only one."

"And I think I can use some of the principles that I applied in Barstow," he said. "Once we knew who Baskin was, then we had to find him. And we did. Probability and elimination."

"Yeah, but we don't have the luxury of time. Once Angel gets his money, he'll disappear. Game over. The only thing going for us is that we've got three agencies with personnel crawling all over the place. I'm hoping he lays low for a few days."

"I'll find him. What kind of a radius do you want?"

"You decide," she said. "He left Santa Fe and went north on 84. Then he took 285 to the east. Then 64 to Taos. I assume the money made it here to Taos. That's where we found the getaway car and the first two bodies of his team."

"Could he have backtracked to Santa Fe after that?"

"Doubtful. At least not very far. From Taos, he continued on 64 to where the accident was. You've got all that info though, right? The accident, the killing of that family. And then Sam getting abducted."

"Yep, I've got it," he said, already tapping away on the keyboard.

"Okay. So I'll leave you to it," she said. "We're going to go over what you found on his background check."

He only nodded, already in a zone as his fingers flew across the keyboard. Cameron backed out of the room quietly, leaving him to it.

"Where's Eric?" she asked as she went back out front, stopping to fill her coffee cup.

"I hope you don't mind, but I instructed him to get a rundown from Samantha Kennedy. Fresh eye, so to speak," Reynolds said.

"We never really finished debriefing her," Cameron admitted as she took a sip of coffee. "Angel had been captured and Murdock all but took us off the case. Since then, there hasn't been time."

"I hope she'll be forthcoming," he said.

"Actually, I think Andi should talk to her."

Andrea flicked her eyes at her and nodded. They'd talked a little about it last night. Sam was very clinical in her answers, not emotional at all. Cameron had suggested that maybe the trauma was more than Sam let on. Maybe she needed to speak with someone. A professional. But Andrea didn't think so. Andrea thought there was tension between Sam and Tori, tension brought on by Angel. She thought that Sam did want to talk but that Tori was too close.

"You think she can get more out of her than Eric can?" Reynolds asked.

"It would be more girl talk and not quite an interrogation," Andrea said.

"I know last night you thought I was being too hard on her. Certainly Agent Hunter did. But we don't really know much about Angel," he said. "Kennedy spent more time with him than anyone else has in years. Anyone that we know of anyway."

"I agree," Cameron said. "But keep in mind she's on our team. You came across as accusing last night."

Reynolds stared at her. "Do you really think it's wise to have her and Agent Hunter still involved in this? Talk about personal," he said.

"Murdock wants Hunter to stay on. He said to cut Sam loose when we get everything we need out of her."

Andrea laughed lightly. "You cut Sam loose, Hunter's going with her. No way Tori stays here without her."

"Orders are orders," Reynolds said.

At that, Cameron also laughed. "Yeah, well, Hunter is kinda like me when it comes to orders," she said.

"She'd risk being reprimanded and possibly losing her job?"

"In a heartbeat."

Reynolds shook his head. "There's no discipline anymore."

Cameron smiled. "At least you're not in a damn suit today." She put her coffee cup down. "Come on. Let's get back to the hotel. We should go over this information that Rowan put together." She turned to Andrea. "And maybe you can slip away with Sam for a bit."

"Yes. If you can keep Tori occupied."

CHAPTER TWENTY-EIGHT

"So he was married?" Sam asked.

"Yeah. Surprised me too," Cameron said. "He never seemed the type."

Sam read through the report Rowan had compiled. It was much more revealing than the one Murdock had given them. The two-year gap that was missing from Murdock's report had him in Spain, living in a small villa near the sea. And married. Wife and son. She nearly gasped as she read the next sentence. *Murdered.*

She glanced up at Cameron who nodded.

"He didn't tell you any of that, I guess."

Sam shook her head. No. In fact, she'd asked him once if he'd ever been in love. Maybe that's why his answer had been so abrupt. His wife had been murdered. Perhaps he tried not to remember that part of his life.

Sam glanced over at Tori, who was watching her intently. She met her gaze, wondering what thoughts were going through her mind. Last night, after everyone had left their room, they'd talked some. But Sam couldn't find the words to explain to Tori how she was feeling. Tori was confused, Sam knew. She also knew how emotionally vulnerable Tori was sometimes. She had seen the doubt in her eyes, and Sam could think of only one way to reassure her. They'd made love with such abandon last night, it had felt almost like at the beginning of their relationship where their hunger for each other could not be satisfied with just one time. Even this morning, the passion was still simmering. Sam had tried to tell Tori without words that everything was okay. That *she* was okay. Tears had come for both of them finally and it was almost a relief to shed them.

Tori pulled her eyes away, looking over at Cameron. "So what's the plan?"

"We wait on Rowan to give us something," she said.

"Like?"

Cameron shrugged. "The most likely places to hide three million dollars."

"How does he even know where to start?"

"Since we don't have a lot of data, he'll use different scenarios," she said. "The programs that Jason wrote hit a lot of different databases so Rowan can pretty much plug in whatever criteria he wants and get some decent returns."

"So we just wait?" Tori asked.

"Afraid so," Reynolds said. "It took some getting used to. But Rowan is very good."

Sam couldn't imagine how they hoped to find Angel using Cameron's computers, but she said nothing.

"I'm in charge of lunch," Andrea said. "I thought burgers." She turned to Sam. "You want to go with me and lend a hand?"

Sam nodded. "Sure."

"I can help too, if you want," Eric offered. "Not much happening here."

Sam saw Cameron and Andrea exchange glances and realized the lunch was staged. Eric had grilled her with questions this morning. She assumed it was now Andrea's turn.

"I think we can handle it," Andrea said to Eric. "Why don't you get everyone's order and email it to me." She held her hands out and smiled. "I will take monetary contributions, however."

Everyone shuffled around as they handed over some cash to her. Sam was about to go to her backpack when Tori stopped her.

"I got it."

Cameron tossed keys at Andrea, who deftly caught them in one hand.

"Be right back."

Sam squeezed Tori's arm as she passed, then dutifully followed Andrea out into the hallway. She was surprised when Andrea leaned closer, a smile on her face.

"I know what you're thinking," she said.

"What? An interrogation is forthcoming?"

Andrea laughed quietly. "Yeah. I figured that's what you thought."

"You mean it's not?"

They walked outside the hotel—the Pueblo Inn. It was an authentic southwestern design, adobe siding and all. Sam thought it was charming and wished they were here under different circumstances. The sky was again cloudless and the air was pleasantly cool with only a slight breeze.

"It's so different from the big city," she said. "I've grown to love Dallas, but I do miss places like this."

"Where are you from originally?" Andrea asked.

"Denver." She shook her head. "And no, I don't get back there often."

"I'm from Los Angeles," Andrea said. "No way would I go back. I met Cameron in Sedona. I loved it there. But traveling like we do now, we've seen so many lovely little towns. I can't decide which one is my favorite."

Andrea unlocked Cameron's truck and they got inside.

"I think I would miss having a home," Sam said. "Do you?"

"Not really. The rig has become home to us. We just change our backyard views quite often," she said with a smile. "Although Cameron has mentioned settling down somewhere."

Sam nodded. After a few seconds of silence, she asked what was foremost on her mind. "So what are we really doing if not an interrogation?"

Andrea looked at her quickly, then turned her attention back to the road. "Honestly? I thought you might need to talk."

Sam was nearly taken aback by the statement. Was she that easy to read?

"If I'm out of line, please say so," Andrea said. "We can get the burgers and go right back. But there's a park a few blocks away. We could sit and talk."

Sam knew the offer was sincere and that Andrea wasn't simply fishing for information—information they assumed she was withholding.

Sam sighed and nodded. "Yes. The park sounds nice."

True to her word, Andrea found the park without a problem. It was small, with only a handful of picnic tables. There was a playground made out of natural materials. No bright blues, yellows or reds to be found. A young mother with two toddlers occupied the swings. She and Andrea walked past them to one of the picnic tables and sat down.

Andrea smiled at her reassuringly. "On the case we had with Reynolds's team, out near Barstow," she said, "I was abducted by our serial killer." She looked away for a moment. "I was bait, basically. We had a tracking device on his truck. And thankfully, also on a watch I was wearing." Andrea looked back at her. "We got in a different truck, so Cameron and Reynolds were following the wrong one."

"Oh, no."

"He was a madman. And I was terrified that I would end up like those women. After he was through with them, he basically euthanized them and then…beheaded them."

Sam shook her head. "I'm sorry. Cameron found you, obviously."

"Yes. But your situation is different, isn't it? I don't think you had that sense of fear that I had." Sam met her gaze and Andrea quickly continued. "I don't mean to imply that you weren't afraid of him. I know how many he's killed. And I assume you *should* have been afraid of him. Only—"

"You're right. And at first, I was." It was Sam's turn to look away. "Tori doesn't understand what's going on with me. And I can't find the words to tell her."

"I can tell there's a little tension between you."

"Yes." Sam smiled at her. "We're okay though. There's nothing that could tear us apart. She's…she's the other half of my soul," she said easily. Her smile faded somewhat. "Angel was never…well, he never physically harmed me. My wrists were tied the first day and I was tied to him. But the more we talked, the less I feared him and the more he trusted me. We shared meals. We gathered firewood. It was almost like we were on a backpacking trip together." Sam blew out her breath and looked at Andrea. "Of course, I knew that we weren't. Should I have tried to escape? Probably. But I was more afraid of the elements, of mountain lions, of getting lost, than I was of him."

"That in itself must have been frightening," Andrea said.

"Yes. Exactly," Sam said. "I questioned myself. I was a cop. Yet I never tried to escape. I never tried to disarm him. I never—"

"From what Cameron said, Angel is too highly trained, Sam. You couldn't have disarmed him."

"I know that. But shouldn't I have at least tried?"

"Look what he did to eight armed men just to escape."

Sam nodded. "Yes. He's killed so many. Yet I wasn't one of them."

"Why do you think that was?"

"Because in that short period of time, we formed a relationship. And he liked me."

"And you liked him," Andrea finished for her.

Their gazes met again. "Yes. I liked him." A smile formed again. "He had these awful beef stew rations," she said. "I hated them. So I asked him to go fishing. And he rigged up fishing gear and he caught a trout. And because he saw how much I enjoyed that, he decided on squirrels the next day instead of the very awful beef stew."

"When we heard those shots, Tori was nearly beside herself."

Sam nodded. "I imagine so." Sam looked away. "I never once considered that. I was happily having dinner, not thinking that she could have heard the shots."

"You feel guilty?"

"Yes. I feel guilty for so much. You were tracking me. Did you take the time for a bath? For a swim? Did you eat fresh trout?"

"No."

"No. And Tori was worried that he was keeping me tied to a tree or something. Worried that he wasn't even feeding me." Sam waved her hand in the air. "And I was acting like I was on a goddamn backpacking trip."

"We all do different things to cope," Andrea said.

Sam's laugh was quick. "Are you trying to make me feel better? This man that I was traveling with had knocked out my best friend. I didn't even know if Leslie was okay or not. Yet I'm following him around the mountain like we're simply out… hiking, for God's sake."

"Sam, you're the only one who can reconcile this guilt that you feel. What I'm trying to say is, you coped the best way you could. And obviously, it was the right way. He didn't kill you."

"But he got away. And then he intentionally drove to a checkpoint. And they beat him up." Sam shook her head. "And I feel guilty for that too. He said he got caught because he wanted to make sure I was okay. And I believe him. I think that's exactly what he did." Sam reached out and grabbed Andrea's arm, tightening her fingers around it. "I should have known he was going to escape. He told me he'd been in worse jams than that. I should have known. I should have said something to Cameron."

"You can't feel guilty over that, Sam."

"He killed eight more," Sam whispered. "*Eight*."

"You can't take the blame for his actions, Sam. You were a victim, too."

"That's just it. I don't feel like a victim."

Andrea's smile was gentle. "Which is at the root of why you feel so guilty."

Sam nodded. "Yes. I know what Tori went through emotionally. I know what Leslie went through physically. Yet I didn't suffer," she said.

"Didn't you? I think you're choosing to forget how you felt when he first took you. You're forgetting the fear you had." Andrea's voice gentled again. "You're suffering right now, Sam."

Yes. She was. But it was a different kind of suffering. She sighed. "Have we accomplished anything?"

"I hope it helped you to say some of this out loud," Andrea said.

Sam gave her a slight smile. "Yes, it has." She reached over and touched Andrea's arm again. "Thank you for talking. And not interrogating."

"Sure." She paused. "Is that what Eric did this morning?"

"He tried. Tori ran interference," she said with a quick laugh.

Andrea smiled too. "Eric is a good guy. He was following orders."

"Oh, I know. He was very apologetic about it. But really, for as much as Angel and I talked, it was mostly personal stuff. He didn't give me any idea of where he might be hiding. Or where the money is. I don't have a clue." Sam sighed. "Reynolds seems to think I'm repressing something. Or intentionally omitting it."

"Reynolds is old school and by the book. Besides, it's personal for him, too. One of the agents killed was a good friend of his."

Sam met her gaze. "You said personal for him too…meaning it's personal for me."

"Isn't it?"

Was that what had her in such a funk? That she felt this whole situation was now *personal* for her? As if she had some stake in it.

Andrea sensed her hesitation, and this time it was she who reached out to touch Sam's arm. "I don't mean that in a derogatory way, Sam. I'm not judging you. But as you said, you feel like you have a relationship with him. The guilt that you're harboring stems from a lot of different avenues."

"Everything that he's done, the killing of innocent people, that family," she said. "Yet I don't want the same to befall him." She shrugged. "I guess I want him to be captured without incident and spend his life in prison." She met Andrea's gaze. "Of course, I know that's not going to happen. He won't be taken alive."

Andrea nodded. "What if Tori is the one to take the shot?"

"I would feel terrible," Sam admitted. "And I would question whether she did it for justice...or if she was simply settling the score with him."

Andrea leaned back against the table, her gaze going to the swing set where the kids were laughing. "When Cameron and I first worked together, I had no idea how Murdock's teams operated. I think Cameron's intention—when we found Patrick Doe—was to kill him without even attempting to apprehend him. I told her I wasn't going to be judge and jury. That's not how I was trained." She turned to her. "But when it came down to it, I was the one who took the shot. And in that instant, I had no thought other than shoot to kill. He had a knife. He had injured Cameron. I *was* judge and jury at that moment. And I took the shot."

Sam nodded sadly. "Yes, when it comes down to it, I guess Patrick Doe and Angel aren't really any different. Does Angel deserve a judge and jury?"

Andrea blew out her breath. "We could say that about so many, couldn't we? I'd like to say we should let our legal system run its course here, but I don't think that will happen. He's killed too many. It's personal for everyone chasing him. So you're right. He won't be taken alive."

Sam nodded again, for she knew Andrea's words to be true.

Andrea stood then and motioned to the truck. "I guess we should get going. I don't know about you, but I'm getting hungry. We didn't have breakfast."

"Me too." And she was. She'd had little appetite lately. She supposed it had been good to talk to Andrea about how she was feeling. She could have told Tori all of these same things, mainly about the guilt she felt. But Tori wouldn't know how to fix it and Tori was all about fixing things. She didn't want to transfer her guilt to Tori.

CHAPTER TWENTY-NINE

Cameron paced beside the table where her phone was, nibbling on a fry as she did. Her burger was long gone. Rowan had texted her, saying he had something. She was waiting on him to call.

"Jesus, how long has it been?"

"Forty-five seconds," Reynolds said dryly. "I'd forgotten how impatient you were."

"I'm just ready to get on with it," she said.

She glanced around the room, seeing Andrea sitting on the edge of one of the beds with Eric. They were sharing fries. Tori and Sam were on the other bed. Sam was still eating her burger. Reynolds was in the chair. He too was still finishing his lunch. She hadn't had a chance to speak with Andi alone, but she could tell that Sam appeared to be a bit more relaxed now. If Andrea hadn't gotten any new information from her, perhaps now Sam would be more inclined for a thorough debriefing. That is, if she could do it without Tori around.

The ringing of her phone brought her attention back to her phone and she snatched it up.

"Took you long enough," she said.

"Sorry. I wanted to compile all three reports," Rowan said.

"Okay. Let me put you on speaker. We're all here." She put the phone down on the table. "Can you hear me?"

"Yes. But we can do this with video if you want. I can link to Reynolds's laptop," he offered.

"Not that I don't want to see your pretty face, but let's just get to it," she said.

"Okay. Well, I tried the obvious links to him. Found two addresses of where he lived as a child. One house has been torn down and a subdivision was built there. The other was a rental house near Angel Fire Resort," he said.

"How ironic is that?" Eric said. "Angel Fire?"

"Yes. That was where they were living when he was born. Makes you wonder if that's how he got his name."

Cameron paced again. "Don't care about how he got his name, Rowan."

"Of course. Sorry." He cleared his throat. "That house is still standing, but it's occupied. It's still rental property. It's been pretty much swallowed up by the resort. The owner won't sell. Well, he will, but he's asking an outrageous amount of money."

Cameron glanced over at Andrea, noting her amused expression. Cameron rolled her eyes.

"Do you have anything useful?" Reynolds asked.

"Those were the only hits on property linking him to this area. Of course, he was twelve years old when he left so I imagine those don't hold much attachment for him. I've found no family that still lives here. His father lives in California as do his grandparents. I've found no evidence that he ever contacts them. His mother's family is gone except for an aunt who lives in Tucson. Again, no evidence that he's been in touch with her in years."

"Okay," Cameron said. "I'm assuming that's only one of the programs you ran."

"Yes. I wanted to eliminate the most obvious. Next, I took a shot at doing what we did in Barstow. Finding abandoned property that has no human traffic. Meaning, abandoned and not for sale. There are too many to name, really," he said. "I've done several different runs. Abandoned property next to other abandoned property. Abandoned property with no close neighbors. There are a few hits, but it's like—"

"Shooting in the dark," Cameron finished for him.

"Right. There isn't enough data to use for any of the algorithms to get a good read."

She sighed. "What else?"

"Well, he had to have done some surveillance of the area at some point."

"Yeah, you don't steal three million on a whim," Eric said.

"We know he got back to the States six months ago. I'm looking through credit card receipts. Gas, hotels, that sort of thing. Starting in Santa Fe and moving up here to Taos."

"How will that help?" Tori asked. "Surely he wouldn't have used his real name."

"Most likely not," Cameron said. "But Rowan might find a pattern with the receipts. That's how we targeted our guy in Barstow."

"Exactly," Rowan said. "The program is running now. It'll take several hours though."

"So basically you're hacking into servers you're not authorized to be in?" Reynolds asked.

Rowan paused. "Yes, sir," he said quietly.

As Cameron was about to speak, Reynolds held up his hand. "I know. I know," he said. "Any means necessary. I just don't happen to agree with it."

Cameron turned toward the phone again. "Well, we've got to do something. Send me what you found on the properties. We might as well take a look at them. We might get lucky."

"I will. I'm also trying to find real-time surveillance video and doing face recognition. I assume the federal marshals and sheriff's department are doing the same thing. I don't anticipate finding anything this early. I think Cameron is right and he might lay low for a day or so. His picture is everywhere on the news."

"Yes, I can't see him feeling comfortable going about town," Reynolds said.

"Okay. Sounds like our best bet is credit card receipts then," she said. "Let me know as soon as you get some data."

"I will. And I'm sending you the list of the properties that I hit on."

"Thanks, Rowan. Good job."

"Sure." He paused. "And by the way, I'm kinda hungry. Is there something here I can eat?"

Cameron looked at Andrea with raised eyebrows.

"Feel free to raid the fridge," Andrea said. "And the pantry."

"Stay out of my beer," Cameron added.

Rowan laughed. "I will."

Cameron tapped her phone, ending the call. She pulled up her email, finding the file from Rowan. "Well, it's not much. Six properties."

"Beats sitting around here," Tori said. "Let's check them out."

"Are we supposed to share any of this data with the other agencies?" Reynolds asked.

Cameron shook her head. "No. Murdock is still trying to swing it so that we're in the lead. So far, no luck. Federal marshals want this guy bad. They feel like they should be in the lead."

"Can't blame them," Andrea said. "I'm sure the sheriff's department feels the same way."

"Yeah, they just don't have the resources to play hardball."

They all stood and Reynolds looked at her questioningly. "Do we split up into two teams or stay together?"

Cameron hesitated. The last time they'd split up, there'd been an explosion and two members of Reynolds's team had been killed. She looked over at Andrea, knowing she was remembering it too. But the reason Murdock had sent in another team was to share the duties. That was why he'd insisted Hunter stay behind too.

"Two teams," she said. "Andrea and Tori will stay with me. You and Eric can take three properties, we'll take three."

Reynolds nodded. "Okay."

"What about me?" Sam asked.

"You're not really cleared to work this, Sam."

"She belongs here as much as I do," Tori said.

Cameron was surprised by her protest. She'd expected Tori to be happy that Sam was going to stay behind, out of harm's way.

"She's not FBI," Reynolds explained. "Goes against protocol."

Cameron laughed. "Yeah, it does, doesn't it?" She glanced at Sam. "Okay. You can come with us."

Sam smiled at her. "Thank you. I'll try to stay out of the FBI's way."

Reynolds simply shook his head as he headed out of the room.

CHAPTER THIRTY

Tori kicked over a rock with her boot, feeling like they were just biding their time until Rowan gave them something more concrete. To say she had little faith in his *algorithms*—whatever the hell they were—was an understatement. Perhaps she'd been with Homicide too long. She was used to beating the streets, interviewing people, looking for clues. She wasn't used to waiting on a computer program to tell her where to look.

"You're frowning," Andrea said. "This isn't your cup of tea, huh?"

Tori turned toward her. For some reason, Andrea could read her almost as well as Sam could.

"No. I'm used to real police work," she said without thinking. Andrea laughed good-naturedly.

"Yeah. Me too. But it's not always like this."

Andrea glanced back at the truck where Sam was waiting. Despite letting her come along, Cameron had been adamant that Sam stay in the truck while they checked the property. Tori thought it was unnecessary—it's not as if they were likely to stumble upon Angel or anything—but at least Cameron didn't insist Sam stay at the hotel. She'd actually given her a job—keep tabs on the chatter between the marshals and sheriff's department. With Rowan's help, of course.

"I guess you two are ready to get out of here," Andrea said.

Tori laughed quickly. "Oh, yeah. It's been a dream vacation so far," she said sarcastically.

Cameron pocketed her phone after ending the call and walked toward them. "They got nothing."

"Were you really thinking we'd hit on something?" she asked.

Cameron shrugged. "Got to check them all out. We got nothing better to do."

Tori sighed. "I know. And one more to go. Where is it?"

They headed back to the truck. "It's the most remote," Cameron said. "A few miles out of town. Pueblo Canyon Road."

Sam opened the door when they approached. Tori shook her head at her unspoken question.

"Did you get with Rowan? Any news?" Cameron asked Sam.

Sam nodded. "They've been fielding hundreds of calls. Apparently Angel has been spotted all over the state."

"Yeah, I imagine. That's what happens when you post his picture all over the damn place."

"Nothing's panned out," Sam continued. "Rowan also said that Murdock was updating the sheriff's department with our progress."

"Progress?" Tori asked. "What progress?"

"He's just trying to pacify everyone," Cameron said. "And not piss them off."

Cameron pulled away from the old, barren house that proved to be as vacant as advertised. Tori had no faith that the third and last one on their list would be any different.

She turned to Sam, who was watching her. She arched an eyebrow and Sam smiled at her. Tori relaxed and let in images of their lovemaking from last night. Sam had been nearly desperate in her touch. It was one of those occasions where they totally connected on every level—body, mind and spirit. It had been so emotional, she couldn't contain her tears. Embarrassed by them, she'd tried to pull back, but Sam held her, silently kissing her tears away even as her own fell. Tori reached over now and took her hand, letting their fingers entwine. Sam squeezed her hand, her eyes softening as they met Tori's. She wondered if Sam was as ready to get back home as she was. Yes, home. And get their life back to normal.

"Did Rowan get any hits on credit cards yet?"

Sam pulled her gaze from Tori and looked to the front. Cameron was watching them in the rearview mirror.

"He said he needed at least a couple of more hours on it," Sam said.

Cameron shook her head. "Supercomputers...you'd think it'd be a little quicker than that."

Sam shrugged. "Just repeating what he said."

"Well, we'll run by this last place, then head back to the hotel," Cameron said. "He should have something for us before nightfall. Maybe the day won't be completely lost."

* * *

Cameron stared in disbelief at the simple dirt driveway that led to the unoccupied—abandoned—house. Tire tracks indicated it might not be so abandoned after all. It couldn't be this easy. She drove past the driveway and parked along Pueblo Canyon Road some thirty or forty feet away.

"Do you think they're fresh?" Andrea said.

"No way to be sure," she said.

She got her binoculars out and focused through the trees, getting a fairly clear view of the house. The windows were covered with blinds or curtains. She could not see inside. On the side of the house, she could make out the back corner of a white car.

"Older model car," she murmured. "Looks like a sedan. Ford or Chevy. I don't see any movement." She handed Andrea the binoculars and took out her phone, calling Rowan. He answered on the second ring. "Yeah, we're at the property on

Pueblo Canyon Road. There's a car in the back. Need you to verify occupancy," she said.

"I triple-checked all the properties I sent you," Rowan said. "It's been empty for over a year. No utilities. No mail service. It's not on the market."

"Who owns it? Maybe they're local."

"Hang on," he said and she heard the quiet tapping on the keyboard. "Owned by Robert Carrillo. Yeah. He lives in Taos."

"Okay. It could be him. We'll check it out. Thanks, Rowan."

"Sure."

She pocketed her phone again. "The owner of the property lives here in Taos," she told them. "That could be him." She then glanced to the backseat where Tori and Sam sat. "You stay put," she told Sam.

"Yes. I know the drill."

Cameron nodded. "It would be too easy if it's Angel. But let's use caution, just in case."

She, Tori and Andrea all pulled out their weapons. Even though they were wearing vests, she still felt exposed. She took the lead, her eyes glued to the house, looking for movement. Maybe it was her imagination, but it seemed unnaturally quiet. Each step they took sounded loud to her ears, the gravel of the road crunching beneath their boots.

"I'm going to go around to the back," she said quietly. "You two take the front. Give me a chance to get back there." She glanced at Andrea, meeting her eyes. "Nice and slow," she murmured.

Andrea nodded.

Cameron walked on, inching closer to the side of the house. Andrea and Tori waited for her to get around, then started walking again. A couple of noisy black and white birds—magpies—were flushed from the trees nearer the road, and Cameron turned quickly, surprised to find three sheriff's department cars skidding to a halt at the edge of the dirt driveway.

"What the hell?"

But she had no time to contemplate it. A single shot from the house—a rifle—shattered glass and the silence was broken.

She saw Andrea and Tori hit the ground and she dove behind a tree as the deputies returned fire, their bullets spraying the house at will. Windows exploded with a deafening roar, and Cameron pulled out her phone as she crawled on her stomach farther away from the house.

Her hand was trembling as she dialed Rowan and she wiped the sweat from her eyes impatiently. She could no longer see Andrea and Tori, but she knew they were caught in the crossfire.

"Rowan…call your contact with the goddamn sheriff's office. Now!" she yelled. "They're firing at our house. Andrea and Tori are trapped. Get them to back the fuck off!"

"I'm on it," he responded immediately.

She disconnected, then called Reynolds. "Get over here!" she said as soon as he answered.

"What the hell's going on? I hear shooting."

"No shit. The goddamn sheriff's deputies are firing at the house."

"What are they doing there?"

"Don't have time to chat, Reynolds. I assume Angel is inside. Someone from the house fired first." She ducked lower as a bullet kicked up dirt not five feet from her. "Tori and Andrea are trapped between them. I need some goddamn help out here."

"On our way."

Cameron rolled over, trying to get a view of Andrea. She heard a car start up and she whipped her head around, just in time to see the white Ford pull away in a cloud of dust, heading up the hill, away from them.

"Goddamn…son of a *bitch*," she muttered.

The shooting stopped almost as quickly as it had started, and silence once again took its place. She sat up, peeking around the tree.

"Andi?" she yelled.

"I'm okay," Andrea called back.

"Thank God," she murmured as she blew out a relieved breath. She stood, holding up her hands as she walked out into the open.

"I'm goddamn FBI," she yelled as she held up her credentials. "Do *not* fire your weapons!"

She saw Sam run up behind the six deputies and pause for only a second before running along the driveway toward the house. Andrea sat up and so did Tori. Even from this distance, Cameron could see the blood. She took off running too, but Sam beat her there.

"Jesus Christ. How bad?" Cameron asked as she stared at Tori, her mouth pulled together in a painful grimace.

Andrea shook her head. "Don't know yet."

"Are you hit?" Cameron asked her.

"I took one in the vest."

"Tori? Jesus, why does this always happen to you?" Sam asked as she knelt beside her. "Talk to me. How bad?"

"Flesh wound," Tori said. "Help me up." Her vest had no less than three bullets in it and blood seeped along her arm. "I think I'm okay." She glanced angrily over at the deputies. "Which one of you *idiots* shot me?"

Cameron's rage boiled over as she met Tori's gaze. She marched toward the deputies, her glare causing several to take a step back.

"You shot a goddamn FBI agent," she yelled, pointing at Tori. "What the fuck were you thinking? This is our goddamn case. Not yours!" She pounded her fist on the hood of one of the cars. "You fucking follow us again, I'll have you thrown in your own goddamn jail," she said loudly.

"Hey, wait a minute. We didn't follow you. We were dispatched," one of them said.

"What the hell are you talking about?"

"There was a nine-one-one call from this residence. Said Angel Figueroa had been spotted here."

"A nine-one-one call?" Cameron slowly shook her head. "Unbelievable," she muttered. She glanced back at them. "So you just didn't see us here or what? You fucking shot an FBI agent."

"How do you know we did? He...he could have," one of the deputies said, pointing at the house.

"No, he didn't." She narrowed her eyes. "If he had shot her, he would have killed her. Now all you've managed to do is let him escape and we're right back to square one." She ran her hands through her hair. "Goddamn it," she murmured. "We had him." She shook her head again. "You're lucky the six of you are still alive."

Before she could say more, Reynolds and Eric pulled up. Reynolds's gaze collided with hers and she shook her head.

"He got away."

"You let him get away?"

Cameron narrowed her eyes. "Don't start with me, Reynolds," she said. "No, I didn't let him get away. These guys were firing on us. Friendly fucking fire. While we're taking cover from these guys, Angel got away."

Reynolds turned to the deputies. "What the hell were you thinking?"

"He fired at us first," one said. "We just returned fire."

Cameron walked away, leaving Reynolds with them. Tori had her vest off and was sitting on the porch of the house. Her T-shirt was shredded. She assumed Sam had torn it and made a bandage.

"Ambulance?" she asked Tori.

"Hell, no," Tori said.

"You've got to have it looked at," Sam contradicted.

"It's fine."

"It's a bullet wound, Tori," Sam said. "Don't argue with me."

"Sam—"

"It's not up for discussion. You *are* seeing a doctor."

Cameron and Andrea exchanged glances, and she nodded at the amused look in Andrea's eyes. It was a conversation that the two of them had had before too.

Cameron left them and walked around the side of the house. Goddamn stupid decision on her part, she knew. If they'd truly thought Angel was inside, how intelligent was it to just walk up like they had? She shook her head. Her gut told her that no way was Angel inside. It was too easy. But she should have been smarter. She should have waited for backup. They should have been sure before just sauntering up like they had.

"Hey."

She turned, finding Andrea watching her. "I'm sorry, Andi," she said. "I walked us right into this. You and Tori, you could have been—"

"But we're fine."

Cameron shook her head. "I just…I just didn't really think that Angel was inside," she explained. "But he's a goddamn sniper," she said, her voice getting louder. "And I walked us right up to the house like we were coming for a visit or something."

"Stop it, Cameron. This isn't accomplishing anything."

Cameron ran her hands through her hair. No. No, it wasn't. Andrea's hands reached out, clasping hers and Cameron allowed this quick moment of contact. They squeezed tightly, saying everything they needed to with that simple touch. Well, almost everything.

"I love you, you know."

Andrea gave her a soft, simple smile. "And I love you."

CHAPTER THIRTY-ONE

Andrea smiled as Sam shook her head disapprovingly at Tori.

"You're so stubborn," Sam told her.

"I've been shot worse," Tori said as she took a seat on the love seat. "It's barely a scratch."

Sam blew out her breath as she glanced at Andrea. "Stubborn," she murmured.

Andrea nodded. "Got one of those myself," she said with a quick smile.

"I know you're not talking about me," Cameron said as she pulled out a beer from the fridge. She held it up toward Tori. "Don't know about you, but this is high on my list right now."

Tori nodded. "Yes, please."

Andrea took the beer from Cameron and walked it over to Tori, then took one for herself. Rowan was still glued to the computers, and Reynolds and Eric had yet to make it over. They were in charge of dinner, and knowing Reynolds, it would be Chinese. She didn't care. She was hungry and would eat anything.

She looked at Sam. "You want a beer? Or wine? Or just plain water?"

Sam smiled. "Something more than water. I'll have a beer too."

Andrea grabbed one more from the fridge and handed it to Sam. Rowan came down the hall, stretching his back.

"So where did Angel go?" Cameron asked as soon as Rowan stuck his head out.

"I'm sorry. I should have seen this," Rowan said. "This would have popped to the top of my list then."

"What?"

"On the satellite, it's nothing more than a trail," he said. "Apparently, it's a crude road cut into the forest. I've traced it and it comes back around to Pueblo Canyon Road. No wonder he felt safe there. He had two outlets."

"Okay, so this was his safe house. But there was no money found there. Nothing inside but water bottles and MRE rations."

Rowan walked over to the fridge, then glanced at Andrea as if for permission.

"Help yourself."

"A beer sounds pretty good right now," he said.

He leaned against the counter of their small kitchen and took a long swallow, letting out a relieved breath and a shake of his shoulders. While they'd been out and about, Rowan had been glued to the computers. No doubt he was as tired as they were.

"Anything on the credit cards?" Cameron asked, not giving him much time to recover.

"Yes, I have something," Rowan said. "It's not quite finished, but I think I've got enough for a profile."

"Great." Cameron moved to her recliner. "Give me something before Reynolds gets here. You know he gets crazy about you hacking into databases," she said.

"Let me get my laptop. It'll be easier," he said.

Andrea sat at the dinette with Sam, but her eyes were watching Cameron. She was pleased to see that she was looking a little more relaxed now. Cameron and Murdock had had a screaming match earlier, so much so that Andrea had to intervene. Yeah, as Cameron had said, if she had to do it over again, she'd have called in the "goddamn National Guard" to surround the house. But really, for them to stumble upon him like they had, no one was thinking about backup. Unfortunately, that wasn't what Murdock wanted to hear.

There was something that was bothering her, though. They had no cover from the house. Two large rocks in front had somewhat shielded them from the bullets flying from the sheriff's deputies, but there was nothing blocking them from the house. Angel would have had a clear shot at them. Yet never once had he taken aim at them. Every shot that came from the house was directed at the deputies. Not them. Cameron's fears were warranted. She and Tori could have been killed. They probably *should* have been killed. Yet Angel never took a shot at them.

She looked at Sam and raised her eyebrows. "You want to take a walk?" she asked quietly.

"A walk?" Sam raised her own eyebrows.

Andrea smiled. "To chat." Then she glanced over at Cameron and Tori. "Alone."

Sam smiled too. "I see." She nodded. "Sure."

They stood at the same time and Andrea looked over at Cameron. "We'll be right back. Just going to get out for a bit."

Cameron frowned. "But Rowan's going to give us a rundown on what he found."

"And when Reynolds and Eric get here, he'll have to do it again," she said.

Cameron nodded. Then…"Is everything okay?"

"Fine. Be right back."

Once outside, Andrea let out a heavy breath. "Sometimes I hate this line of work."

"Me too."

"The more I think about it, settling down in some sleepy little mountain town—where the most excitement is a drunk and rowdy Saturday night fight—is sounding better and better."

Sam smiled. "Is that in your future?"

"I know when Cameron first mentioned it, she probably wasn't thinking of that as an immediate option," she said. "But after all this, I think we might have a serious discussion about it."

She led them down the narrow road, past other RVs and campers. As had most of the days been, it was clear and pleasantly cool, another gorgeous early autumn day.

"I really hope Tori leaves the FBI," Sam said. "I knew she didn't have the camaraderie there that she had with Casey and John, but she led me to believe she liked it there. It was a bit of a shock to hear she was thinking of going back to Homicide."

"Were you surprised she hadn't said anything to you?"

Sam nodded. "We don't keep things from each other. We talk about everything. Knowing Tori the way I do, I imagine she wanted to be sure before she mentioned it to me."

"So her mentioning that she's thinking about it means she's already made up her mind?" Andrea guessed.

Sam laughed. "Yes. I'd guess that as soon as we get back to Dallas, she'll contact Lieutenant Malone." Sam turned to her. "But is this really what you wanted to come out to chat about?"

Andrea shook her head. "No. I guess I was musing on life after the FBI." She took a deep breath. "Something I've not mentioned to Cameron, but…Tori and I…we were in Angel's direct line of fire out there. And not once did he target us."

"Are you sure?"

"Yes. I mean, it was chaos out there and I know it only lasted sixty seconds or more, but the shots he fired from the house were aimed at the deputies, not at me and Tori. I remember thinking, who do we take cover from?"

"You were on the other side of the rocks," Sam stated.

"Right. The rocks were between us and the deputies. There was nothing between us and the house. Of course, once the shooting started, there wasn't any time to do anything other than what we did, which was to get as low as possible and cover our heads," she said. She felt a chill as she realized just how vulnerable they'd been.

"So what are you thinking?"

Andrea turned to her. "It's a little crazy."

Sam met her eyes. "You think he intentionally spared you because of me?"

Andrea nodded. "He knows Cameron. He doesn't know me or Tori."

"Yet he knew one of you must be Tori, my partner."

"Yes. And he didn't want to kill her." Andrea shrugged. "And if I told Cameron this, she would indeed say it was crazy. Angel is a killer. He doesn't *spare* people."

"He spared me," Sam reminded her. "But it wasn't something I had considered. I mean, I thought you were taking fire from both sides. It was a miracle you didn't get hit."

"I took one to the vest, Tori took three. All from handguns. Angel was using a rifle." She paused. "But the miracle, as you call it, was Angel's humanity. For whatever reason, the bond you two formed while out there is strong. And he knew that if he killed Tori, that would crush you. So he spared both me and Tori." She took a deep breath. "And that's a little scary to think about," she admitted. "And Cameron beat herself up pretty bad over it too."

"What do you mean?"

"Us going to the house like we did, without backup."

Sam nodded. "Yes, you were exposed. What do you think would have happened if the deputies hadn't shown up? What do you think Angel would have done?"

"I honestly don't know. I can't see him letting us get close. Maybe he would have fired a few warning shots, enough for him to get to his car."

"Well, none of us expected him to be there in the first place," Sam said. "I mean, what are the chances Rowan pulled six properties off a list and we get a hit?"

Andrea smiled. "I know you and Tori don't understand his method or even how the algorithms work, but he simply pulled the top six that had the highest probability," she said.

"According to a computer," Sam said with a shake of her head.

A honking of a horn startled them and they moved out of the way, only to see Eric grinning at them from behind the wheel of their rental.

"You gals need a lift?"

"Depends," Andrea said. "You got food in there?"

CHAPTER THIRTY-TWO

Cameron used the plastic spoon to scoop out more rice, adding it to her spicy shrimp and vegetables.

"You gonna eat that last egg roll?" Tori asked, already reaching for it.

"Yeah, I am. Get back," Cameron said as she slapped at Tori's hand.

"Jesus, you'd think it was a slice of pizza or something," Tori murmured, causing Andrea to laugh.

"If it had been the last slice of pizza, I would have stabbed you with my fork," Cameron said as she took a loaded bite with rice and shrimp. She saw Andrea and Sam look at each other and smile, and she gave a subtle wink to Andrea.

The motorhome had been crowded with all of them inside so they decided to take their early dinner out to the picnic table. Reynolds and Eric had supplied them with a variety of Chinese dishes and a platter of egg rolls. Conversation had been light and meant only as filler. They hadn't discussed the episode at the house at all. And Rowan had only given her the bare minimum on his credit card search. From what he'd told her, though, he had enough to piece together a pattern.

Reynolds wiped his mouth with a paper napkin, then took a swallow of water from his bottle. Cameron met his gaze across the table and knew he'd reached his limit on downtime.

"I haven't spoken to Murdock," he said. "I assume you have."

Cameron nodded. "Oh, yeah. It wasn't pretty," she admitted. "Apparently we should have *known* it was Angel at the house and should have called in every law enforcement officer in the whole goddamn state as backup and then nuked the house off the face of the earth," she said. "With Angel still inside, of course."

"Easy to second-guess now," he said, surprising her. "If I had been in the lead, I would have done the same thing. It wasn't as if you drove right up to the front door."

She put her fork down, still eyeing the egg roll. She shoved it over in front of Tori, who quickly snatched it up. "Yeah, I know," she said to Reynolds. "But still, I should have taken more precaution. Checking these properties out was more an exercise of killing time until Rowan could get us something a little more concrete," she admitted. "I never really thought it was Angel inside the house."

"I'm surprised none of the deputies took a hit," Eric said.

"Me too," Cameron said. "With Angel's skills, he should have been able to take all six of them out."

"It didn't really last all that long," Andrea said. "A minute, tops." Then she raised her eyebrows almost apologetically. "Of course, being caught in the crossfire, it seemed like an hour."

"I second that," Tori said. "But you're right. He fired a lot of rounds from the house in that long minute. Their cars were shot to hell, but none of them even had a scratch."

Cameron saw Andrea and Sam exchange glances once more. She was again curious about what they talked about on their walk. But rather than ask them point-blank in front of everyone, she thought she'd save it for tonight, when she and Andrea were alone.

"If I didn't know better, I'd say Angel wasn't shooting to kill," she said.

Sam nodded. "I agree. It was only a distraction." She glanced at Reynolds. "If I may interject here, that is."

"By all means," he said.

Sam leaned her elbows on the table, glancing at all of them before speaking. "He used the word 'distraction' quite a bit. Whether he originally planned to…to eliminate his whole team or not, I don't know," she said. "But when the two guys tried to double-cross him and take the money, he killed them. I don't know if that's when the other three became expendable or not. But everything else he did after that was solely for a distraction. Causing the accident that closed the road, killing that family." She glanced over at Tori. "And even taking me. It was all just a distraction." Sam turned to Cameron. "Why would today be any different? Maybe he saw us drive up. He knew every law enforcement agency in the state was looking for him. So a quick call to nine-one-one sends the sheriff's department racing over."

"And there was just enough of a distraction for him to slip away," Cameron said. "I didn't even come close to taking a shot at him. I was too busy dodging bullets of my own."

"That's all well and good, but where the hell is he now?" Reynolds asked.

Cameron turned to Rowan. "You're up, kid. Tell them what you found."

Rowan nodded. "Well, keep in mind it's nothing concrete. And I'm still running two programs." He moved his plate aside and pulled his laptop in front of him. "But I think it's substantial." He glanced quickly at Reynolds. "I compiled data using credit card receipts," he said. "We know he surfaced again here in the States six months ago. I used that as my starting point. Basically, I grabbed any transaction made after that date within a hundred-mile radius of both Santa Fe and Taos."

"That had to have been thousands of transactions," Tori said.

Rowan shook his head. "Oh, way more than thousands," he said. "Hundreds of thousands. I kept gas and fuel transactions separate for my first search, then combined that with the returns on food, lodging and well…basically everything else."

"Yeah, great," Cameron said. "Tell them what you found."

"I found two patterns that fit. One occurred five months ago. The other, just one month ago."

"What kind of pattern?" Reynolds asked.

"The first one, Charles McDaniel. He used a credit card to rent a car in Albuquerque. Gas receipts show he traveled back and forth between Santa Fe, Taos and Eagle Nest for nearly a month. Unfortunately, there were no hits on that credit card for lodging or meals."

"Okay, you're saying that's the only person who traveled that same route during that time?"

"No. But what I was able to match was another credit card—Justin Black—used in the same vicinity at the same time. In fact, several fuel stops charged to Charles McDaniel's card also had food charged to Justin Black's card nearly simultaneously."

"So your theory is that Angel had these two cards, used them at will without fear of being tracked?" Tori asked. "Wouldn't it have been safer for him to use cash?"

"Why use his own cash when he can charge to a false account?" Cameron asked.

"Isn't he taking a chance that these guys know their cards have been compromised?" Tori shrugged. "As careful as he's been, this seems reckless."

"They're not real," Rowan said. "Well, the cards are real, but they're forged," he explained. "Identity theft. By the time Justin Black and Charles McDaniel were made aware of the charges, he had already ditched the cards. The only hits were just in that one month."

"Okay," Reynolds said. "What else? Surely this isn't all you have. I mean there is no way this proves that it was Angel using the cards. And even if it did, it doesn't help us find him."

"Five weeks ago—the same pattern, different cards, different names," Rowan said. "Only, there were added stops. Lodging and fuel hits near the armored car company. And there were two car rentals this time, not just one. The second one was in Santa Fe."

Tori shook her head. "Okay, maybe I'm just not seeing it, but what the hell does this prove? And how the hell does it help us?"

"It's not black-and-white," Cameron said. "If you put in the data and get returns, you've got to trust it. I know it doesn't make sense."

"Say I trust it," Tori said. "Now what? What does it do for us?"

"I'm running car rentals within the last month," Rowan said. "We know he had a getaway car, we know he had a car stashed in the mountains. And now we know he's got a white Ford."

"Maybe he bought them," Sam said. "Not rented."

Rowan nodded. "Yes. Maybe he did. I'll run that too. I'm also doing a search on those two names to see if anything pops up."

"What else are you running? You said you had a couple of things still going," Cameron said.

"Property in the Taos area that's been purchased or rented in the last six months. Hiding in abandoned property is one thing, but wouldn't he feel safer if he had his own place?"

Reynolds shook his head. "That makes no sense. He steals three million dollars. Wouldn't he just take the money and run? Besides, if he's got his own place, why did we find him at an abandoned property?"

"Because his picture has been plastered all over the news," Sam said. "If he does have a place, it's most likely in a public area. Maybe even an apartment."

"I think if he does have a place, it wasn't part of the original plan," Cameron said. "Yes, take the money and run makes the most sense. But he's no longer operating under that plan. He's on Plan C, at least."

Reynolds stood, pacing behind the picnic table. He shook his head again. "Conjecture. Nothing more than assumptions and conjectures. I have to agree with Agent Hunter. This doesn't help us. We're no closer to finding him." He looked at Cameron. "So we had a pattern? It tells us what he did, not what he's going to do."

Cameron smiled. "You know me, Reynolds, I'm all about speculating."

"Actually, two patterns," Rowan corrected him. "And I'm still running credit card transactions, looking for something during the last two weeks to current."

"He was here five weeks ago," Andrea said. "Isn't it safe to assume he never left?"

"The credit card hits lasted three weeks, then stopped," Rowan said.

"So he's got more cards. Or maybe he started using cash," Eric suggested.

"Well, we know he's got three million dollars now," Tori said.

"Look, before we all get discouraged by this, let's let it play out," Cameron said.

"What's there left to play out?" Reynolds asked. "We have nothing. We're sitting around here with our head up our asses doing nothing," he said, his voice getting louder.

"We're doing what we do," Cameron said calmly. "If the federal marshals are beating the streets or the sheriff's department is beating the streets…that's what they do. That's not what we do. We let Rowan do his thing. When he gets something, we'll check it out. Just like we did today." She paused. "Like we worked it in Barstow," she said.

Reynolds stared at her, still slowly shaking his head. "We missed him today. That was probably our only shot. My guess is he's long gone from this area by now."

"Not without the money," Sam said.

"After everything that happened today, you still think he's hanging around?"

"Yes. Otherwise, what was the point of it all?"

CHAPTER THIRTY-THREE

"I'm so ready for this to be over with," Andrea murmured against Cameron's lips.

"Me too."

Cameron kissed her again, but when the kiss deepened, Andrea pulled away. They didn't have time.

"Rowan will be back soon," she said.

Cameron sighed. "I know. I'm also ready to get our house back."

"You're the one who agreed to let him sleep here tonight," Andrea reminded her.

"The sooner he finds something, the sooner we can get out of here," she said. Cameron grabbed her hand and pulled her closer again. "Are you okay?"

She nodded. "Yes. Why do you ask?"

"You were kinda quiet today. I know the thing at that house—"

"I'm fine, sweetheart. Quit beating yourself up over that." She met her gaze. "Besides, I don't think we were ever in any danger from Angel."

Cameron frowned. "Is that what you and Sam went to talk about?"

Andrea smiled, wondering when Cameron would bring that up. She tugged Cameron down beside her on the love seat, moving Lola into her lap. The purring cat stretched out, then crawled over to Cameron's lap instead. Cameron immediately plunged her fingers in Lola's black fur.

"Angel never took a shot at us," she said. "And it couldn't have been that he was too concerned with the deputies to worry about us. We were in his line of sight."

"So what's your theory?"

"He didn't want to kill Sam's lover."

Cameron shook her head. "No. That's not how it works, Andi. The Angel I knew, he was by the book when it came to this. There are only two concrete rules—accomplish the assigned mission and get out alive. Everything else is simply collateral damage. No matter what it is," she said. "There can't be any type of emotional attachment in his line of work. Angel doesn't care about that. He wouldn't care that Tori might be out there. He's a killer."

"I disagree," Andrea said. "At least in this case. He *does* care. He cares about Sam. For whatever reason, he does."

"So you think because Tori was there, he wasn't shooting at you?"

"Yes. He could have killed us. He could have killed all six deputies, if he's as good as you say he is. But he didn't. No one was killed." She met Cameron's gaze. "The Angel that you knew, he would have killed them, right?"

"Yes."

"So maybe Sam is right. Maybe it was simply a distraction. Maybe his true mission here is the money, nothing else. He's not just shooting to kill every time he tries to—"

"Distractions are one thing, Andi. But killing that innocent family? Killing eight law enforcement officers to escape?"

"There's your collateral damage. He was escaping. His goal is the money. That's it."

"So are you saying he didn't shoot you because Tori was there or he didn't shoot you because there was no need to? That he only needed to distract us long enough to get away?"

Andrea smiled. "Maybe a little of both?"

Cameron smiled too. "Maybe. And I guess we'll never know."

Headlights flashed outside and a few seconds later, Rowan was knocking on their door. Andrea took Lola as Cameron got up to let him in. He had a small duffel bag, which he tossed on the floor beside the love seat.

"I'll get you some sheets," Andrea offered as she made her way into their bedroom.

Cameron and Rowan went into the small office, and she tuned out their conversation as she mindlessly went about unfolding the love seat and making up Rowan's bed. She got the coffeepot set for the morning, then ducked into the bathroom. When she came out, Cameron was waiting.

"Ready for bed?"

Andrea nodded. "Yes. It's been a long day."

Cameron nodded. "Yeah, it has." She motioned to the bedroom. "I'll be right in."

Andrea touched her arm as she walked by her, squeezing lightly.

"Goodnight, Rowan," she called as she passed the office.

"Night," he said, never taking his eyes from the monitor.

* * *

The incessant beeping finally penetrated her sleep. Cameron rolled over, blinking several times before it registered. Andrea was still fast asleep, one hand curled around Cameron's arm. Cameron reached for her phone. It was nearly four. She gently moved away from Andrea and slipped from the room. She pushed the office door open, the beeping louder now. She stared at the flashing on the monitor's screen for a moment. Apparently Rowan's programs had run their course. Hopefully, they had hit on something.

She went into the living room and paused, smiling as she watched Rowan in sleep. He was curled into a ball, looking much like a young boy instead of an FBI agent. She reached out and touched his shoulder lightly.

"Hey...wake up."

He jumped, his eyes wide. "What's wrong?"

She held her hands up. "Nothing." She motioned down the hall with her head. "Your program's finished. The alert is going off."

He rubbed his eyes, then swung his legs off the bed. She stifled her laugh at the Batman-themed underwear he wore. He covered them up as he hurriedly stepped into his jeans.

"What time is it?" he asked as he slipped his glasses on and shuffled into the office.

"Early," she said. "Four."

He turned back to look at her. "Coffee?" he asked around a yawn.

She nodded, knowing she would not go back to sleep. "Yeah. Coffee." She took a moment to glance at the closed bedroom door where Andrea and Lola were still asleep. She sighed, wishing she could go back in there and join them. But no. Coffee. Time to get to work.

Cameron went into the small office with two steaming cups of coffee. Rowan didn't seem to notice her approach.

"You take it black, right?"

He looked up then and nodded. "I think I found him."

Cameron's eyebrows shot up as he took the coffee cup from her. "You think?"

"Five months ago, utilities were turned on in a rental house. Maria Joseph."

"That means what?"

"Maria was his wife's name. Joseph was his son."

Cameron stared at him. "That's it? That's what you got?"

"I put in everything we know about Angel Figueroa. All the data that I have on him. This rental property is at the top of the list. I'm running a cross-check now, but Maria Joseph doesn't appear to exist in the Taos area at all until five months ago."

Cameron ran her hand through her hair. "I don't know, Rowan. Seems a little improbable, doesn't it?"

"I thought you didn't believe in coincidence?"

She nodded. "You're right. We need to check it out. Who owns the rental property?"

"It appears to be an individual. Margaret Torres. I've got her info."

Cameron nodded. "Okay. I'll call her. See who this Maria Joseph is." She sighed. "At a reasonable hour, of course." She took a sip of her coffee. "What else you got?"

He shook his head. "Nothing else that ranks as high."

"Shooting in the dark," she murmured.

"Needle in a haystack," he countered.

CHAPTER THIRTY-FOUR

Sam moaned quietly as Tori's mouth moved lower. Tori nudged Sam's legs apart with her knee as she captured a nipple between her lips. She had no idea what time it was, but Sam's hands had been caressing, urging her to wake. When Sam had whispered "make love to me," Tori had rolled them over, her own hands moving across Sam's naked body.

"Yes…with your mouth," Sam murmured.

Tori smiled against her breast, then moved lower still, her lips wetting a path along Sam's stomach, pausing to nibble at the hollow of her hip, relishing the familiar taste of Sam's skin. But Sam's hands pushed her lower and Tori let Sam guide her. It was dark in the room, but Tori knew her way well.

She spread Sam's legs even more, then buried her face between them, her moan mixing with Sam's as her tongue snaked through her wetness. The past week had put a strain on their relationship but this…this, at least, felt normal. There was no manhunt for a killer, no FBI team, no strange hotel room. Not now. Now, there was only the two of them…making love.

Tori closed her mind to everything else as she drew Sam's clit into her mouth. Sam jerked her hips against Tori's head as her tongue flicked back and forth, just like she knew Sam loved.

"God...yes," Sam breathed. "Don't you dare stop."

Tori had no intention of stopping, not even when her phone rang. Sam's hands clutched her shoulders tightly and Tori ignored the offending sound of her phone, listening instead to Sam's rapid breathing and quiet moans. But the phone didn't stop. The ringing started again after only a moment of silence.

"Don't even *think* about answering it," Sam murmured.

But the ringing continued, and Tori nearly growled in frustration. She pulled away from Sam, reaching for her phone.

"It's Cameron," Tori said to Sam as she checked the phone. She rolled onto her back, her breathing as labored as Sam's. "This better be important, Cameron, because your timing sucks," she said bluntly.

Cameron laughed. "Sorry. I don't even want to know what I interrupted. But Rowan has something. I've already called Reynolds."

"Okay." Tori sighed and glanced at Sam, who still had her eyes closed.

"You've got at least a half hour before Reynolds and Eric will come looking for you. That should give you enough time to finish whatever it was I interrupted," Cameron teased. "And by the way, pick up breakfast on your way."

"I hate you," Tori muttered before she hung up.

Sam rolled her head toward her, a smile on her face. "You two are so much alike."

"Like hell we are," Tori said. Tori rolled toward Sam and pulled her close. "Now...shall we continue?"

Sam kissed her and nodded. "Please do."

* * *

"McDonalds? You got McDonalds?"

"I didn't pick the place," Tori said as she bit into her breakfast sandwich. "Reynolds was driving."

"Figures," she said as she too took a bite.

"Can we get on with it?" Reynolds asked impatiently. "Rowan? What did you find?"

"Rental property," he said, glancing at Cameron. "Cameron called the owner first thing this morning."

Cameron nodded. "Yeah. Rowan found a rental house that had utilities turned on five months ago."

"What does that prove?" Reynolds asked.

"Nothing, really," she said. "The name was Maria Joseph." She shrugged. "Could be anything."

"His wife's name was Maria," Sam commented.

"Yeah. And Joseph was his son's name."

"I'm assuming this is more than a coincidence then?" Reynolds asked.

"I called the owner of the house," Cameron said. "Nice lady. Very forthcoming with information. She said a man rented the place for his niece. She never met him. Did everything over the phone. He paid her six months' rent in advance. Paid cash."

"Still inconclusive," Reynolds said.

Cameron glanced at Rowan. "Not really."

"The man's name was Charles McDaniel," Rowan said.

"The name on the credit card," Eric said, nodding. "Not a coincidence."

"Wait a minute," Tori said. "If he had this house all along, why the hell did he hide out at an abandoned property?"

"I don't know," Cameron said. "Maybe he was just trying to lay low for a while. This rental property is in a residential area. Since his face has been all over the news, maybe he didn't want to take a chance on being seen."

"Have you contacted Murdock? We should get the other agencies involved," Reynolds said.

"No way," Cameron said. "Do we want another incident like we had at the house?" She shook her head. "We do surveillance, we do a stakeout."

"I think we should—"

"Reynolds, it's a residential area. You get a hundred cops out there, what do you think is going to happen?"

"What does Murdock say?"

"He says it's my call," Cameron said. "It'll be a goddamn bloodbath if we storm the place."

"If we surround the house, give him no escape route, then—"

"Angel won't go down without a fight," she said.

"Then what do you suggest?"

Cameron glanced at Sam, then at Reynolds. "We need to take him out. Quietly. Not give him a chance to kill anyone else."

"Make him the target?"

"Yes."

Reynolds eyed her. "And you'll do this?"

Cameron let out a deep breath. She'd long ago given up her role as a sniper. But when she'd spoken to Murdock earlier, they agreed that trying to take him by force would only result in more deaths. There had been enough killing. There was only one more person who would die. And that was Angel Figueroa. So she nodded, taking the time to look at each of them. Andrea acknowledged her decision with a subtle nod, and she was surprised that Sam did as well.

"Okay. Then what's our plan?" he asked.

"We'll do like we did at that old waterpark in Barstow. Go in after dark. Wireless earpieces and wrist mics again," she said. "Rowan's been working on it already."

"What about surveillance?" Eric asked.

"I've put together a series of satellite images of the area," Rowan said. "You can get familiar with it and decide how you want to stake it out. It's an older neighborhood. One thing that probably made it appealing to him is that there are very few streetlights. None near the house."

"We'll need another car," Cameron said. "I want three posts. I think we can cover several blocks and still be safe." Cameron looked at Sam. "And I think you should stay here with Rowan."

"No," Sam said with a quick shake her head. "I understand this is an FBI mission, but I'm going with you. I'll stay in the car like before, but I'm going."

Cameron had figured that would be the case, but she thought she would suggest it anyway. So she nodded, then pointed at Eric. "I'll leave it to you to get us another car."

"You got it." Eric paused. "Will we use the thermal imaging like we did in Barstow?"

"We'll need to, yes. It'll probably be the only way I get a clean shot," she said. She glanced over at Tori, who had been exceptionally quiet, then to Sam. "I know this seems nothing like police work," she said. "But we've been given the go-ahead to take Angel out. I'm not really crazy about it...but it is what it is."

Sam met her gaze head on. "If you're giving a disclaimer on my account, don't bother. I know what the situation is."

Cameron nodded. "Just so you know, we did toss around the idea of you negotiating with Angel."

Sam gave her a half smile. "I don't think that would make any difference."

"No. Probably not."

CHAPTER THIRTY-FIVE

Tori shifted in her seat as Cameron pulled to a stop a block and a half from the rental house.

"Appears to be the same white Ford," Eric said.

Tori touched her earpiece, pushing it more securely into her ear. "Wonder why he didn't ditch the car?" she asked.

"Maybe he thought it was safer to keep it than try to get another one," Cameron said.

"How long do we wait?" Reynolds asked.

"Full dark," Cameron said.

Tori leaned back in the seat and tried to relax. Full dark would be another twenty minutes, at least.

The house was on a corner lot. The neighborhood was older and appeared to be mostly rentals. The nearest streetlight was two blocks away. Past the house in the opposite direction, Reynolds and Eric were parked. And down a side street, behind the house, Andrea and Sam were in the new rental car Eric had picked up. She and Cameron had a visual of the house and she assumed Eric and Reynolds did too.

Tori had really hoped that Cameron would insist that Sam stay behind. Hell, she had mentioned it herself, but Sam had been adamant about going. Tori wasn't sure if it was because Sam wanted to be there in case something happened to *her* or if Sam wanted some sort of closure because of Angel. She knew Sam was harboring some guilt over Angel's escape. If things worked out the way Cameron planned, this whole thing would be over with tonight. And soon.

"I can't get crap with this thing," Cameron said. "We're too far away from the house to zone in."

"The thermal imaging?" Eric asked.

"Yeah. Hell, I'm picking up signals from all over. The neighbors appear to be having dinner," she said.

"Why did you let Eric have the night vision goggles?" Tori asked.

"Because she's got that toy," Eric answered. *"I'll need to get closer too, though."*

Cameron held up the monitor for her to see. "I think this might be the house," she said, pointing to a cluster. "If so, there's more than one person in there."

* * *

Andrea glanced over at Sam who had become increasingly quiet. Her blond hair rustled in the breeze as she continued to stare out her opened window. They had turned their mics off when they'd first headed out and conversation between them had come easily. She found Sam to be quite engaging, and she knew that if given the chance, they could become friends.

But there was one thing they had not mentioned. The plan was to take out Angel. Plain and simple. Sam had been noncommittal during the planning stage for tonight's mission, simply listening and not contributing. Part of that, of course, was that she was not FBI and not really a part of the mission. Andrea wondered if there wasn't more to it.

"Do you have reservations about all this?" In the shadows, she could barely make out Sam's expression, but she saw her nod.

"I'm a cop," Sam said. "Only on TV is the only option shoot to kill."

"I know what you mean," Andrea admitted. "I told you how I felt about being judge and jury. It's not something I believe in. And for all of Cameron's bravado, she hates it too. Her training, her experience in the military has prepared her for this, though." She sighed. "It's disturbing to think that we're staking out this house, waiting to move on it so that we can kill him instead of capture him."

"Yes, it is. It seems so far removed from law enforcement," Sam said.

Andrea nodded. "Murdock's teams *are* far removed from it. I've only met Reynolds's team, not the other. I know Cameron, of course. And Reynolds, he would never take advantage of the carte blanche Murdock gives them. But I would imagine it puts a lot of pressure on Murdock to make sure he has the right people on his teams."

"And not have someone who thinks they are always above the law? Yes, I guess it is a fine line to walk." Sam tilted her head, watching her. "Do you think that may be why Cameron is ready to settle down and leave the FBI?"

"I think that's part of it, yes," she said. "And I think she genuinely wants a house, wants to put down roots somewhere. She grew up in a military family. She's been in the military her whole life. I think she's ready to settle down."

"Does she have a family? Siblings?"

Andrea shook her head. "No. She doesn't have family." She paused, wondering if Cameron would mind her telling Sam about her father. It wasn't something Cameron ever talked about. "Her brother was in the military too. He was killed," she said. "And…well, her father, he was also in the military. He found her mother with another man, an officer. He killed them both."

"Oh, God."

"So he's in prison." She decided she wouldn't mention the fact that Cameron's father had kidnapped her and taken her into the wilderness in Canada to avoid capture.

"You're her family then," Sam said. "Tori doesn't have any family either. Her father was a cop too. A home invasion...well, her whole family was killed. I hate to think about it, and Tori doesn't talk about it, but the guy killed everyone but Tori. He left her tied to a chair at their dinner table, all her family dead around her. I think she was twelve years old."

"God, how did she mentally survive that?"

"She used to think she hadn't," Sam said. "She lived with a very loving aunt and she helped her heal. She wanted to become a cop so that she could solve her family's murder."

"No one was ever arrested?"

"No. And after all this time, I think she's resolved herself that no one will be."

"That's got to be very hard for her."

"Yes. But we've made a home, we are our own family. And Casey and Leslie, they're our best friends. Casey and Tori are like sisters."

"With our lifestyle now, that is the one thing I miss," Andrea confessed. "Friends."

"Another reason to settle down," Sam said. She paused. "It's odd how similar their lives have been, isn't it? I mean, minus the military, of course."

"Yes. Maybe that's why they're so much alike."

Andrea settled back in her seat, enjoying the coolness of the evening. She could hear the breeze stirring the leaves on the aspen tree they were parked under. Daylight had dwindled and she could no longer make out the subtle gold color that was just starting to show. She knew from their travels in the west that they were missing the peak color by about two weeks. Maybe when this was over, Cameron would want to head up into the mountains again.

* * *

"Hey guys," Eric said. "There's a black Mustang cruising by. That's at least the third time I've seen it."

Cameron and Tori looked at each other. "Surveillance," they said at the same time.

"Goddamn," Cameron murmured.

"*It's pulling in the driveway,*" Eric said, his voice low.

Cameron felt her adrenaline kick in, and she squeezed her hand around her rifle. She knew it was too dark to take a shot. Not from here.

"Can you see?" Tori whispered beside her.

Cameron shook her head.

"*Okay, it's not Angel,*" Eric said. "*Judging from the looks of him, I'd say a local thug.*"

"I've got to get closer," Cameron said. "I can't tell how many people are in the house from here."

"*I've got eyes on the door. All is quiet now,*" Eric said.

"He's put no lights on," Tori said. "He's got to know we're here."

"If he hired a local and that was indeed surveillance, then yeah, he must suspect we're here," Cameron said.

"*Are you ready to call for backup?*" Reynolds asked.

"Yeah, let's shoot up the whole goddamn neighborhood, Reynolds."

"If not backup, then what do you suggest?"

"How about…'FBI. Come out with your hands up!'? You think that'll work?" She heard nothing but a quick laugh from Andrea. Reynolds didn't bother to reply. She glanced over at Tori. "Everyone is so uptight."

Tori raised her eyebrows. "Plan B then?"

"Do we have a Plan B?"

"*We wait him out,*" Reynolds suggested. "*He's got to come out sometime.*"

"*We still don't have a positive ID that Angel's even in the house,*" Eric said.

"I've got to get closer," she said again. "Let me see if I can pick something up with the thermal imaging."

"*Be careful,*" Reynolds whispered.

Even though it was a pleasant evening and a light breeze was blowing through the open truck windows, she felt perspiration trickle down her neck. She got out quietly, making sure not to close the door. She had already turned the interior lights off.

"*I see light inside,*" Eric said. "*Looks like maybe the kitchen window. It's over here by the carport.*"

"*Looks like a flashlight,*" Reynolds said.

"Copy that," Cameron whispered as she pressed up against a blue spruce that separated the two houses. She held the device out, making sure to stay in the shadows. She finally got a reading and was shocked to see four people inside. "Got four inside," she said.

"*Makes no sense,*" Reynolds said. "*He's on the run. He's been all over the news. Who in their right mind would team up with him?*"

"*He's got three million dollars,*" Tori said. "*Money talks.*"

Cameron crept back to the truck and slipped inside again. She tossed the device on the seat with a heavy sigh. Four? Who were they and how well trained were they?

"What are you thinking?"

She turned to Tori. "I'm wondering if these are local thugs, like Eric thinks, or if these are part of his team. Maybe a second team he had lined up, just in case." She held her wrist mic closer to her mouth. "Sam? What do you think?"

There was only a slight pause before she answered. "*I don't think he had any other team here,*" Sam said. "*He was used to working alone. I don't think he would trust that many people.*"

"I suppose if he had another team, he would have called them in right away," she said. "So if they are locals, we can assume they aren't well trained."

"*So what do you want to do?*" Reynolds asked. "*I still think we should wait them out.*"

"Wait them out? Wait for them to come out?" she asked. "So if he comes out with his three friends around him, do I just take them all out? Or do we let them get in the car and have a chase?" She ran a hand through her hair in frustration. "Hell, maybe he gets away long enough to take another hostage. Maybe we can play that game all over again."

"*What the hell is wrong with you?*"

"I'm tired, Reynolds. I'm frustrated. And I'm sick to death of Angel Figueroa."

"I'll second that," Tori said quietly beside her.

Cameron closed her eyes. She needed to focus. She couldn't be tired. She couldn't be frustrated. She couldn't be at the point where she was ready to just walk away from it all. She allowed herself a glimpse of the future, with she and Andrea in a little mountain town, maybe living in a cabin. Hell, maybe getting a dog or even another cat.

"Cameron?"

It was Andi, and she smiled, recognizing the gentle tone of her voice. How did Andrea know that she had reached her limit?

"Yeah, I'm okay," she said, answering her unasked question. She cleared her throat. "Okay, let's talk this through. Does he know we're out here? Was the guy in the Mustang doing surveillance? Angel is smart. He's leaving nothing to chance." She paused, feeling out of sorts. "We could wait, as Reynolds suggested. Maybe I could get a shot when he comes out. But if I don't, then what?"

"They're inside the house," Eric said. *"We don't have to lay low now. Let's get closer. It doesn't have to be you to take the shot if we're nearer the house."*

"I agree," Tori said. "The last thing we need is to let him get back inside his car."

"Are we willing to chance one of these other three guys being causalities?" she asked.

"If they're mixed up with Angel, they're not innocent," Reynolds said. *"We can assume all three of them are armed."*

Cameron blew out her breath. She didn't like it. They were leaving too much to chance and Angel was too good. Maybe she should have done what Reynolds suggested in the beginning— surround the goddamn house. But Murdock had agreed with her. There was just too great a chance of the neighbors getting caught in the crossfire.

"I got a bad feeling," Tori said beside her.

"Yeah. Me too."

"*Do you want me come up from the back like we planned?*" Andrea asked.

"Yes. Sam…you stay in the car."

"*I will.*"

"Okay. Nice and easy, everyone. Be sure of your target."

CHAPTER THIRTY-SIX

Andrea opened her door, then closed it soundlessly. Before she could walk away, Sam called out a quiet "Be careful," and Andrea paused and nodded.

"I will. Thanks."

Sam watched her until she disappeared into the shadows. She touched her earpiece, but all was quiet from the others and she assumed they were moving into position. She felt helpless—useless—out here but knew this was an FBI mission and she had no part in it. Her main goal was to stay out of the way. She knew, of course, what the outcome would be. She only hoped it would end quickly. However, she had a feeling it wouldn't. So far, nothing had gone as planned.

She found herself tapping her thigh nervously with her fingers, and she finally opened the door, stepping outside into the cool night air. She paced aimlessly, back and forth, waiting for something to happen.

"We're beside the house," Eric said quietly.

"Let me see if I can get a reading on their positions," Cameron said.

Sam looked to the sky, seeing an endless array of stars overhead. She blew out her breath, knowing it could all be over within a few minutes.

"What the hell? I've only got three now," Cameron said.

"Maybe you had a false reading earlier," Reynolds said.

"No way."

"The only doors are the front and the one at the carport," Eric said. *"No one has come out."*

"There are goddamn windows at the back, aren't there?"

Sam listened to their exchange, frowning slightly as the possibility sunk in. It was then that she felt, rather than saw movement beside her. She turned and gasped as Angel stood not five feet from her, his gun pointed at her.

"Angel."

"Hello, Sam." He walked closer. "Lose the weapon," he said, pointing at her holster.

She held her hands up, staring in disbelief at him. "What... what do you want?"

"The weapon, Sam. Toss it on the street." He came closer still, his gun pointing directly at her face. "Now."

* * *

Andrea turned, one hand pressed against her ear, shocked by what she was hearing. *Angel.* She ran back toward the car, trying to ignore the others as their voices all sounded in her ear at once. She could no longer make out Sam's voice over the others, and she had no idea what was happening. As she caught sight of the car, she saw Angel shoving Sam inside through the passenger's door. She skidded to a halt and took aim, firing without thinking. She saw Angel flinch, then saw him turn in her direction. Gunfire erupted and she dove behind a parked car, covering her head as the windows were blown out, spraying glass all around her. The roar of the engine and squeal of tires had her bracing as the rental car bumped the fender of the car she'd taken cover behind.

As soon as it pulled off down the street, she stood, aiming but didn't fire. She couldn't take a chance on hitting Sam.

The chatter in her ear became nearly unbearable, but she did notice that Sam's voice was absent. Had Angel found the mic? The earpiece?

"Reynolds, find out who's in the goddamn house!" Cameron yelled. *"Call for backup."*

"Sam! Sam! Are you there?" Tori pleaded.

Andrea heard tires squealing and knew Cameron and Tori were on their way. She walked over to where the rental car had been parked. Broken glass littered the street and her boots crunched across it. She flashed her light around, stopping when she saw blood. Not a lot, but enough to know she'd hit him. She bent down and picked up Sam's weapon, tucking it into her jeans at the waist.

She looked up as a truck sped her way, and she stepped aside as Cameron pulled to an abrupt stop.

"What the hell happened?"

* * *

"Turn here…to the left," Angel said.

Sam took a chance with a quick glance in his direction. He was still holding the gun on her, but his other hand clutched his stomach.

"Are you hit?"

"Just drive."

"Angel, are you hit?" she asked again as she turned the corner

He didn't answer, but she could tell his breathing was labored. She gripped the steering wheel hard, trying to decide what to do. Would he really shoot her? After all this, would he really shoot her?

"Why are you doing this, Angel?"

He slumped back against the seat. "I'm sorry, Sam. Sorry for all of it."

She recognized the pain in his voice. "How bad are you hit?"

"Yeah, she got me pretty good," he said. "Was that your Tori?"

Sam shook her head. "No. That was Agent Sullivan. Andrea," she said.

"What's with all these women agents?" he asked. "But no, I didn't think that was your Tori."

"Angel, let me take you to the hospital," she said.

"No, Sam. That's not how it's going to end."

He leaned his head back, and she glanced at him again. The gun was no longer pointing at her, thankfully. He still clutched his stomach and in the dim light from the dashboard, she could see blood covering his hand.

"It's not too late."

"It is too late. Far too late," he said. "I'd rather die than spend my life in prison." He turned toward her. "There's a road up ahead. A forest road. Take it to the right."

"Where are we going?"

"I'm taking you to the money," he said. "Do you have your cell on you?"

She hesitated. If she said yes, would he toss it out the window like he'd done the mic and earpiece?

"Yes," she finally said.

"Good. Then they can track you."

* * *

"Let's go already," Tori said as she paced beside the truck.

"Go where?" Cameron said as she motioned down the street.

Andrea heard sirens in the distance and knew that the shots had been reported. Porch lights had popped on all over, and she could see people coming out of their houses, no doubt wanting to see what was going on.

"Come on, Cameron! We've got to do something," Tori said loudly.

"We don't know where he went," Cameron said just as loudly. "Let me think."

Andrea let her fingers circle Cameron's arm tightly. "Track her cell phone," she said.

Cameron nodded. "Yeah. That would be too easy, wouldn't it?" She took her phone out and walked a few paces away. "Rowan? Angel's got Sam. I need you to track her cell. I'll bring it up on the truck's console, like we did in Barstow." She paused. "And get some backup out here for Reynolds and Eric."

Andrea turned to Tori. "We'll find her."

Tori shook her head. "That goddamn bastard. I can't believe he's got her again."

"For what it's worth, I don't think he'll hurt her."

Tori stared at her. "You don't know that."

"I think Sam knows that."

CHAPTER THIRTY-SEVEN

While the forest road was a decent gravel road, the one he directed her down now was bumpy and uneven. She heard him moan in pain as they hit a hole.

"I'm sorry," she said.

His jaw was clenched and his breathing ragged. "Just a little farther. It's an old hunting cabin," he said. "My dad used to come up here with some of his buddies. Hunting was the excuse for coming here, but all they did was drink."

"Who owns it?"

"Not sure," he said. "It looks like it hasn't been used in twenty years or more."

She slowed her pace even more as the road all but disappeared. The lights cut through the darkness, through pines and scrub oak and the ever-present smattering of rocks.

"Are you sure this is the road?"

"There's a little opening to the right," he said. "The cabin is beyond that."

She slowed to a crawl, finally seeing the opening he was talking of. "Will the car make it?"

He didn't answer, and she turned down the little path. The trees scratched the car as she squeezed through, then her headlights found the cabin he was talking about. It appeared to be little more than a shanty. She turned to him, but his eyes were shut, his face etched in pain. The gun lay beside him on the seat, and she knew she wasn't in any danger, if she'd ever been.

"Angel?"

His eyes opened, and he blinked several times. "Help me out, please," he said.

She nodded, then hurried around to the passenger side to help him. He made no attempt to take the gun. She took his arm and looped it around her shoulder. He slumped heavily against her, and it was only as they walked into the light that she saw how badly he was injured. Blood covered his shirt and jeans, and she stared as it still seeped between his fingers.

"Oh, Angel," she said quietly. "Why won't you let me take you to a hospital?"

"No."

He shuffled on, and she supported his weight as they went to the door. A new padlock held the latch in place.

"Key is in my right pocket," he said.

She separated enough from him to find the key. It was on a small key ring sporting a bright yellow smiley face.

"Really?"

He tried to laugh. "My attempt at humor, yeah."

She unlocked the door and pushed it open.

"There's a flashlight on the shelf, just to the right of the door."

She felt along the wall, touching the shelf. She found the flashlight and turned it on. She flashed around the cabin, seeing that it was only one large room, nothing more. Against one wall were several duffel bags.

"So yeah, that's what three million dollars will fit into."

He moved toward the opposite wall, and she helped him to it, then he slid down until he was sitting. He leaned back, again closing his eyes.

She let the light settle on him, shocked by the amount of blood she saw. His face was pale and he was sweating, one hand still pressed against his stomach. His eye was still discolored from the beating he'd taken, but it wasn't nearly as swollen as it had been. But still…

"Jesus," she whispered. "I can still call an ambulance, Angel."

"No. I won't go to prison." He tried to smile. "God knows I deserve it. But it ends here, Sam."

She shook her head sadly. "I'm sorry."

"Don't you dare," he said. "You have nothing to be sorry for. I'm the one who is sorry." He looked up at her. "Come sit. Talk to me."

* * *

"Step on it, will you?"

"Goddamn it, Hunter, I'm driving as fast as I can."

Tori clutched the dashboard as Cameron turned a corner, skidding as the paved road became gravel.

"It's not fast enough."

"Why don't you just watch the console and make sure I don't take a wrong turn."

"We don't even know if the phone is still on Sam," Tori said. She watched the blinking dot which hadn't moved in the last ten minutes. "Hell, he could have tossed it. It's stationary."

"I realize that," Cameron said. "Rowan's already sifting through satellite images, looking for outbuildings."

Tori pointed to the console as they approached a road to the right. "Turn here."

Cameron did, and they immediately hit a hole, bouncing them all in the truck.

"Is this even a road?" Andrea asked.

"We're close," Cameron murmured.

"I don't see any other roads. There's nothing else on the map," Tori said.

"Then they're on a trail or something. We're close."

* * *

Sam sat down beside Angel, leaning back against the wall much like he was. She put the flashlight on the floor and its beam casts its light on the duffel bags. She took his other hand and held it, feeling his fingers tighten around it.

"Thank you."

"Are you in a lot of pain?"

"Not too bad. It just feels numb," he said.

She turned away from him and stared at the money instead. "Why three million dollars?"

"Because…I wanted out of this life. I wanted to start over."

She looked at him again. "Tell me about your wife."

His eyes opened and he met hers. "So you know? Is that how you found the rental house?"

She nodded.

"My only love," he said. "Maria. But I guess you know how that ended."

"Just the facts. Not what really happened," she said.

His eyes closed for a moment. "I wanted a normal life. When I got out of the military, I just wanted…normal. I fell in love. First and only time. We had a son. Joseph. We had a good life," he said. "We lived by the sea and I worked on a boat. I fished. It was a simple life." He turned his head toward her slightly. "But this man, he wanted me to work for him. He had a list of high-profile enemies he wanted killed. Enemies he couldn't get close to. I could."

He paused for a long time, and she didn't think he would continue. "What happened?"

"I refused to work for him," he said. "When I got home one day…well, I found them. They had been butchered. My Maria and Joseph. And he called me up, asked if I was ready to work for him now."

"So you ended up working for him anyway?"

"No. I went to his mansion and I cut his throat and I watched him bleed out."

"Angel...I'm so sorry."

She saw tears in his eyes as he struggled to continue. "My world fell apart then. I had nothing. I had no heart. I had no soul. So I did the only thing I was trained to do. Kill. My life was never the same. It was just empty...and so, so lonely," he said, his voice barely more than a whisper.

She felt a tear run down her cheek, and she wiped it away. "I wish things were different," she said. "Another life, another time, I think you and I could have been good friends."

He smiled and nodded. "Yes. I believe so. Other than Maria...you are the closest thing I've had to a friend," he said.

"Is that why you spared me?"

He nodded. "Something about you, Sam, touched me inside. I'm not sure what it was, but I couldn't harm you. You have an innocence about you. I think you reminded me of Maria from the start."

She shook her head. "Not so innocent. I'm a cop. I've seen far too much to still have innocence."

"You may think you're jaded, but you're not. I see a gentle sweetness...an innocence in you...I couldn't take that from you." He coughed several times. "Maria was such a good person. Full of light, never darkness. I see that in you too."

She felt the strength leave him as his hand loosened around hers. She didn't know what to say to him, and she couldn't stop her tears. But his fingers tightened around her hand once more.

"Don't cry for me, Sam. I don't deserve your precious tears."

She wiped them away impatiently. "I'm sorry. I can't help it."

"No. I know you can't. I've done such horrible things... yet the goodness in you...well, you're still trying to find the goodness in me. It's futile. I'm afraid there isn't any."

"I don't believe that."

He squeezed her hand again, then let his fingers loosen. "Thank you for being here with me...now." His voice was barely more than a breath. "I'm not in pain, Sam. Not really." He struggled to talk, to breathe. "It isn't a...a bad way to die."

She stared at him, tears still streaming down her cheeks. She watched as his eyes clouded over and he seemed to drift away. His hand went limp as he took his last breath...then nothing. He was still.

She wiped her tears away, embarrassed for having shed them. She reached out and closed his eyes, then moved away from him.

She pulled her shirt out of her jeans, using the end to wipe her face, her nose. Just like that, it was over with. She took a deep breath.

Angel was dead.

She picked up the flashlight and pulled her cell out of her pocket, intending to call Tori. But before she could, she heard a truck and saw headlights flash outside. Angel had been right. They had found her. She pushed the door open, recognizing Cameron's truck. But to be sure, she held her hands up as she walked into the light.

"Sam?"

"I'm okay," she called.

Tori was in the light, but Cameron stopped her before she could come closer.

"Angel?" Cameron asked.

Sam gave a quick shake of her head. "He's...he's dead," she said, motioning inside.

Cameron let her arm fall from Tori, and Tori hurried over, wrapping her in her arms. Sam sank into her embrace, knowing that this nightmare was finally over with.

Tori pulled away, watching her. "Blood? What happened?" she asked as she wiped at Sam's face.

"No. Not mine," she said. "I'm fine. He was...he was wounded. Badly."

She turned to Andrea, who met her gaze. Andrea shook her head slowly.

"I'm sorry, Sam. I should have—"

"No. You did everything right," Sam said. She walked closer and hugged her tightly. "Thank you, Andi." Then she smiled at her. "May I call you Andi?"

CHAPTER THIRTY-EIGHT

Cameron's light flashed across the room, landing on Angel's body, which was slumped against the wall. Blood soaked his shirt and jeans. She walked over and squatted down beside him, touching a finger to his neck. His skin was still warm, but she felt no pulse.

"So that's Angel?"

Cameron turned, finding Tori in the doorway. She stood and nodded. "Yeah. That's him."

"I'm not sure what I was expecting," Tori said.

"A monster, perhaps?"

Tori still stared at him. "Yeah. A monster. He looks like a normal, clean-cut guy."

"He was still a monster." Cameron went over to the duffel bags and opened one. "Jesus, Hunter...you ever seen this much cash?"

Tori shook her head. "How many people died for this?"

"Too damn many."

Cameron zipped it back up and tossed it aside, then opened another one. It, too, was stuffed with cash. She assumed they all were. Her phone broke the silence and she snatched it up.

"Reynolds? How did it go?"

"We're okay. Eric was right. They were locals. Angel gave them some cash to canvass the area and to run interference for him. When they spotted us, he slipped out a back window."

"Any fireworks?"

"No. Hell, they nearly pissed in their pants." He paused. "Sam? She okay?"

"Yeah, she's fine. Angel is dead."

"Good. And the money?"

"It's here. Not that I know what three million dollars looks like, but there's a hell of a lot here. We're in a cabin of some sort, out in the woods," she said. "I'll have Rowan run GPS on us. Now that it's over, Murdock will probably get the Albuquerque office involved again." Or at least she hoped he would. She was ready to put an end to this case.

"You want us to come out there?"

"Yeah. And bring some pizza. I'm starving."

CHAPTER THIRTY-NINE

"I can't wait to get out of here," Tori said as she shoved what few clothes she had into the backpack Casey had left for them.

"Yeah? You're not going to miss Cameron?"

"Hardly." But she added, "I guess she did kinda grow on me, though. And I really liked Andrea."

Sam nodded. "Yes. Andi's nice. I think if we all lived in the same area, Cameron and Andrea would fit nicely into our little circle of friends."

Tori laughed. "Casey would drive Cameron crazy. Of course, I can't see them in a city. Can you?"

"No. They seem to be pretty much at home living out of an RV." Sam raised her eyebrows. "What about you? Ready to be back in the city?"

"Yes. Aren't you?"

Sam walked closer and looped her arms around Tori's neck. "I'm just ready to be home. I'm ready to get our life back."

Tori ducked her head, kissing Sam slowly, thoroughly. Yeah, she was ready to get their life back too. She pulled away, meeting her gaze. "Are you okay? I mean, with…"

"I'm fine. I knew what the outcome would be, Tori. I just didn't anticipate being there when he died. It was…emotional."

"I know he got inside your head, Sam."

Sam nodded. "Yes, he did. But in a good way, Tori. And honestly, I'm glad I was there with him when he died. I understand him better." Sam turned away from her. "I know he was a killer, I know what all he did. But I understand the why of it now." She looked back at her. "It doesn't make what he did right, of course." Sam took a deep breath. "But I'm glad it's over with. And I hope I don't ever have to go through anything like that again."

"You and me both."

Sam smiled and nodded. "So? What's the first thing we're going to do when we get back?"

"I want to eat Tex-Mex. Let's go to O'Connor's favorite place and get chicken enchiladas and a Rios Rita," she said, already imagining biting into the spicy enchilada. "I can't believe we've been in New Mexico and have *yet* to eat Mexican food."

"Tired of pizza?"

Tori laughed. "God, Cameron and her pizza. I think I've had enough to last me a year."

Sam smiled at her again. "I spoke with Leslie earlier."

"Oh, yeah? How's she doing?"

"Good. She's going back to work on Monday."

"That's great."

Sam squeezed her hand. "She also said that Casey was hinting to Malone that you wanted to go back to Homicide."

Tori rolled her eyes. "She wasn't supposed to say anything."

"Does this mean you've made up your mind?"

Tori tilted her head questioningly. "What do you think I should do?"

"Well, I know you haven't been happy with the FBI, even though you never said anything," Sam said.

Tori nodded. "I miss the team, yeah." She met Sam's gaze. "Do you think Malone would bring me back?"

Sam smiled and leaned closer, kissing her. "According to Leslie, they've already got your old desk ready to go for you.

Besides, I can only imagine the trouble you and Casey will get into as partners."

Tori laughed and pulled Sam into a tight hug. "You're right. And yeah, I've already made up my mind. I want to go back."

"Good. Then let's go home."

* * *

Cameron paused at the highway, looking to the right where they would take Highway 64 into the mountains of Colorado. She glanced over at Andrea, who sat with Lola in her lap. She took her hands off the steering wheel and sighed.

"I'm tired, Andi. Tired of this life."

Andrea smiled at her. "Yes, I know you are, sweetheart. So where do you want to settle? What sleepy little mountain town do you want to call home?"

Cameron shrugged. "Maybe we don't have to settle down right away. Maybe…we could…you know, buy our own RV. We could travel with the seasons. I wouldn't mind spending the winter on some beach."

"So this life you're tired of…it's just the FBI, not traveling?"

"This case took its toll on me. Chasing Angel through the mountains on foot—hell, I'm not as young as I used to be."

"Is that all it is, Cameron?"

Cameron shook her head. "No." She sighed. "I don't feel like I have the drive anymore. I'm tired of it all. I'm tired of guns, of violence. I want some peace. I don't want to have to dread it every time the phone rings and wonder where Murdock is going to send us next."

Andrea reached across the console of the motorhome and laid her hand against her thigh, squeezing lightly.

"Then let's do it. We've got quite a bit of money in savings," Andrea said. "The last few years, it's not like we've had living expenses." She smiled. "Well, other than pizza."

"Very funny." Cameron covered Andrea's hand with her own. "Do you mean it? You want to go see the sights with me? Be tourists for a while?"

"Yes. I'd go anywhere with you, Cameron."

Cameron brought Andrea's hand up and kissed it gently. She'd been so afraid Andi would say no.

"So we'll travel around and when we find the perfect little mountain town, we'll settle. How's that?"

Andrea laughed. "Sounds like a plan."

"Good." Cameron finally pulled the rig out onto the highway, feeling free. "Now we just have to tell Murdock."

"I'm going to miss the motorhome though."

"We'll get another one, just not this big." Cameron chanced a quick look at her. "Can I get a dog too?"

Andrea's eyebrows shot up. "Do you think Lola will allow that?"

Cameron's gaze settled on Lola, who was perched importantly in Andrea's lap. The black cat turned and pierced her with what appeared to be accusing eyes.

"Probably not," she said with a laugh. "I think we'll get one anyway."